E. Harris Smith Calder, Joseph Thomson

Ulu

Vol. 2

E. Harris Smith Calder, Joseph Thomson

Ulu
Vol. 2

ISBN/EAN: 9783337347253

Printed in Europe, USA, Canada, Australia, Japan

Cover: Foto ©Andreas Hilbeck / pixelio.de

More available books at **www.hansebooks.com**

U L U

AN AFRICAN ROMANCE

BY

JOSEPH THOMSON

AUTHOR OF "THROUGH MASAI LAND," AND "TO THE CENTRAL AFRICAN
LAKES AND BACK;"

AND

MISS HARRIS-SMITH

IN TWO VOLUMES.—VOL II.

LONDON:
SAMPSON LOW, MARSTON, SEARLE, & RIVINGTON,
LIMITED,
St. Dunstan's House,
FETTER LANE, FLEET STREET, E.C.
1888.

LONDON: PRINTED BY WILLIAM CLOWES AND SONS, LIMITED,
STAMFORD STREET AND CHARING CROSS.

U L U.

CHAPTER I.

At daybreak next morning the Kennedys and their guest foregathered to discuss an early cup of coffee, in the cool, easy dress permitted by custom in tropical climes.

" Has any one seen Ulu this morning ? " asked Kate, suddenly, in the midst of the light talk which ensued. " Ferjallah, do you know where she is ? " she continued, addressing the boy in attendance.

Scarcely had the words left her lips when a sharp, ear-piercing scream quivered through the air. For a moment every one sat still, each looking at the other in mute surprise. Again the scream broke upon their startled ears.

" What is it ? " cried Kate, springing to her feet

and rushing towards the door, to be simultaneously followed by Mr. Kennedy and Gilmour, who feared they knew not what.

Outside they found the entire settlement assembled in bewildered, panic-stricken groups, every one excitedly demanding of his neighbour the cause of the agonized cry. "El-Masai!" "Robbers!" "Buffaloes!" "Lions!" were the terror-striking words that passed from lip to lip, each new suggestion only serving to intensify the general uncertainty and augment the hideous din.

On the appearance of the wazungu the clamour increased tenfold.

"Kélélé!" (Silence) commanded Gilmour, sternly. "Is there any one missing?" he asked, as soon as he had obtained quietness.

For a moment no one spoke. Then one of Kate's small boys raised a trembling voice, and said that Ulu had gone outside the village that morning, and had not returned.

"Has no one seen her?" cried Gilmour, with a scared look.

An eloquent silence told its own tale.

"My rifle—quick!" he went on, turning to Uledi. "Come now, boys," he added, as the weapon was promptly placed in his hand; "follow me. There's no time to—— Good heavens, Miss Kennedy, where are you going?" he broke off abruptly, aghast at finding Kate, carried away by a generous impulse to help, instinctively running with him towards the gate.

Gilmour's astounded look and question, added to her father's exclamation of amazement and alarm, at once brought the impulsive girl to a recollection of her uselessness, and she stopped suddenly short, not without a strong feeling of rebellion at her woman's weakness and helplessness. "What would I not give to be a man?" was her mental ejaculation, as she stood enviously watching Gilmour's retreating figure and longing for his power of action.

Meanwhile, following the direction from which the shriek seemed to have proceeded, Gilmour plunged into the banana grove, a number of men close behind him.

"Stop!" cried Uledi, suddenly, before they had proceeded many yards.

"What is it?" asked Gilmour, eagerly.

"Look!" returned Uledi, briefly, as he pointed with his finger to the ground.

"Simba!" (lion) was the exclamation that broke simultaneously from all as they recognized the well-known footprints in the mud. A look of blank consternation spread through the crowd—a lion or a Masai were two things no M-Chaga could be brought to face.

"Go on, Uledi—quick!" said Gilmour, in a low tone of suppressed excitement. "We must make haste."

With body bent and eyes eagerly scanning the pathway, Uledi took up the trail and moved swiftly forward in the direction of the jungle. A few steps further and all doubt as to Ulu's possible fate was removed. First came traces as of a body having been dragged along the ground; next a prettily beaded sandal was picked up and recognized by Gilmour as one his little *protégée* had worn; finally, to inflame his already excited feelings still further, several drops of blood were discovered on the fallen leaves. Happening to look round at this point, Gilmour found that the greater number of the Pisgah men had disappeared. Calling a halt, he sternly demanded of those who remained if any were afraid, conjuring all such in God's name to go back now.

The two Wa-Swahili who constituted Gilmour's own private following needed no words to express their feelings in the matter; their faces spoke their eagerness to press forward. Encouraged by their fearless demeanour, the Pisgahites assumed a bold front, declaring that they laughed at lions and would follow Gilmour to the death. Though somewhat doubtful of the sincerity of their devotion, there was nothing for it but to accept their

assurance, and once more Gilmour gave the order
to go on.

So far their way had lain through the banana
trees, where they felt comparatively secure, it
being possible to see some distance ahead. Now,
however, the trail suddenly left the pathway, and
diverged into a dense jungle. This was more than
the Pisgah men had bargained for, and for a
moment even upset the equanimity of Gilmour
himself, the impossibility of keeping an effectual
look-out enhancing the dangers of the enterprise
tenfold. Nevertheless, he plunged boldly into
the tall grass, closely followed by the two Wa-
Swahili and one or two of the less cowardly mission
men.

Now began the dangerous part of the chase.
The sole hope of succouring Ulu depended on the
possibility of advancing without a sound. There
were no longer any footprints to serve as a guide
to the whereabouts of the lion; an occasional drop
or splash of blood alone told of the path he had
taken. Throwing themselves flat on their faces,
Gilmour and his little party wriggled noiselessly
along, with growing assurance that their game
must be near, and proportionate heightening of the
excitement. At every sound they stopped to listen
with bated breath and straining ears. Slowly and
with redoubled caution they approached the centre

of the jungle, prepared each moment to come face to face with their expected prey. With a sudden presentiment of evil, Gilmour looked sharply round to see if his men were all right. To his unbounded rage and dismay, he found that the men from the mission station, utterly terror-stricken, were meditating flight; which would mean that the lion would be immediately apprised of their presence. Gilmour was equal to the occasion. With a look that meant mischief, he whipped out his revolver and made a significant motion. Helpless and speechless, the cowards collapsed, and Gilmour, his fears for the present allayed, ostentatiously handed the revolver to Ferhani, with a silent hint how it was to be used in case of need.

Once more the slow creeping was resumed. Inch by inch they progressed, every sense on the alert, every rifle held ready for instant action. The moments seemed like minutes, and the excitement grew painful to a degree. At any instant the little band might be upon the lion, or, what seemed equally probable, the lion be upon them. The suspense became unbearable, and in the uncertainty of his position Gilmour again felt that strange impulse to inaction with which doubt can shake even the bravest heart.

But the crisis of the enterprise had arrived. Noiselessly pushing aside the tall grass, preliminary to advancing the next few inches, Gilmour found himself face to face with the object of his anxious chase. With a start he drew back, letting the grass close over him again. An admonitory kick served to apprise Uledi that the supreme moment had come. Firmly grasping his rifle, Gilmour cautiously rose to his knees, and once more parted the grass in front of him. There lay the lion, in all his tawny magnificence, couched in a small open space not two yards away. At first, Gilmour could perceive no trace of Ulu. Then, half-hidden by the brute's great heavy body, he noticed a dark rounded arm, which the lion was licking with a peaceful, satisfied air, apparently whetting his appetite with the blood which trickled slowly from an ugly wound a little below the elbow.

Boiling with rage and grief, our hero pushed his rifle through the grass and took aim. Another second and the lion would have been no more; but ere Gilmour could draw the trigger, a sudden swish of bushes behind him, followed by a revolver-shot, so disconcerted him, that off went both barrels at once, unfortunately injuring nothing save Gilmour himself, who received a severe shock from the re-bound. Startled by the report, the lion rose in all its majesty, its grand, shaggy head erect, its eyes gleaming with royal fire, its tail extended and waving gently from side to side; while on the ground beneath lay little Ulu, all-unconscious—a pedestal for the fore feet of the beast of prey.

In its first moment of startled indecision, as it stood uncertain where to spring upon the intruder, the lion presented a capital chance for a shot; but Gilmour's rifle was empty, and, spell-bound by the spectacle before him, he neglected at once to lay hold of the big elephant-gun Uledi promptly pushed towards him. The lion's hesitation was short-lived. Attracted by the movement of the grass caused by the flying mission men, it rushed towards them swift and straight as an arrow. Roused by the sight, Gilmour sprang to his feet, gun in hand. There was no time to raise his weapon to his shoulder, or in any way to take aim. The brute's hot breath almost reached him as he simultaneously fired both barrels. In its recoil the gun struck him right in the chest, laying him on his back devoid of wind and senses. Missing him in its spring, the lion rolled over him with a terrible roar of rage and pain, knocking down Uledi, and landing at the feet of Ferhani, who fell back with amazement, but instinctively discharged shot after shot into the dying brute, as it rolled about in terrific convulsions, tearing up the ground with its claws, and gnashing with its teeth whatever it could lay hold of in its fearful agonies. The struggle, however, was short. Before Uledi had time to recover himself and seize his rifle, the lion lay quiet in death. Assured of their safety, Uledi next hurried to his master, though himself bleeding from a wound made by the lion's claws as it threw him down. He soon found that he had nothing to fear on Gilmour's account. Almost before he could reach him his master had recovered consciousness, scrambling to his feet in a dazed sort of way, and hastened towards Ulu, who lay apparently dead. For a moment it seemed as if Gilmour's worst fears were realized, and as he knelt down to place his hand over the little maiden's heart, he was conscious of a strange lump in his throat and a strange dimness in his eyes. To his intense delight, he could still feel a tiny flutter of life.

" Water—quick ! " he shouted eagerly, springing to his feet and tossing his hat to Ferhani, who ran with all speed to fill it at a neighbouring canal. Again kneeling beside her, Gilmour dashed some of the cool liquid on Ulu's unconscious brow. The next moment a slight tremor passed over her, her bosom heaved, and, with a low plaintive moan, she slowly opened her eyes. Swallowing a little of the water, she recovered still farther, bestowing a look of mute gratitude on her preserver, who now busied himself binding up her bleeding arm.

Just as Gilmour had successfully extemporized a bandage with his handkerchief, a great commotion arose outside the jungle. Emboldened by the sound of the rifle-shots, and safe in the conclusion that the lion was now powerless to do them hurt, the mission men appeared in force, with renewed display of wordy valour.

"Where is the lion?" they shouted as they approached. "Show us the lion that we may kill it!" and on they rushed pellmell to where the royal brute lay dead. Like curs they precipitated themselves on the carcase, loading it with opprobrious epithets and treating it with all the vehement obloquy of which craven souls alone are capable.

With a look of disdain, Gilmour turned his back upon the contemptible spectacle, and bade Uledi and Ferhani carry Ulu to the mission-house without further delay. Obedient to his orders, they gently lifted their unresisting burden, and with firm, regular tread began to retrace their steps through the now well-trodden grass. Gilmour himself walked alongside, ready to render assistance if necessary; while the noisy crowd, already tired of their cowards' sport, quickly fell into procession behind, and, dragging the dead lion in their midst, triumphantly proceeded towards the village with much victorious shouting and singing of songs.

CHAPTER II.

As the jubilant crowd emerged from the banana grove they were met by every woman and child in the settlement, and by every man whom age, fear, or weakness had forced to remain behind. Miss Kennedy alone was absent. Disgusted with the desertion of the mission men, whose untimely return had proclaimed their cowardice, and impatient at the conduct of the women, who were all more bent on selfishly knowing themselves secure from the lion than ready to exert themselves on behalf of Ulu or any who might have sustained injury in going to her assistance, Kate had returned to the mission-house, there to make such preparation as she was able for the reception of possible sufferers. Apprised of the return of the rescue-party by the exultant shouting of the crowd, Kate hastened to the porch, where she was in part relieved of her anxiety on seeing Gilmour and his servants coming slowly along the pathway towards her. Running out eagerly to meet them, her heart beat more anxiously as she perceived their apparently lifeless burden; for Ulu, weak from loss of blood and overcome by the pain of her wounds, had again fainted.

"Is she much hurt?" asked Kate in a low tone, her cheek paling with fear of what might be the answer, as Gilmour stepped out in advance to meet her.

"Her arm is badly lacerated, and she has lost a good deal of blood; nothing worse, I think."

"Bring her to the house at once," said Kate, addressing Uledi and Ferhani; and, without stopping to waste time on further questions, she turned and made all speed towards the porch.

"This way, please," she said, as, entering the sitting-room and passing swiftly through it, she raised the curtain which separated it from an adjoining chamber—her own bedroom, as Gilmour afterwards learned. "Now, lay her on the bed," Kate went on, as the men entered and stood waiting to receive her orders. "There, that will do," she added; and, only stopping to pull the pillows from beneath Ulu's head, so as to facilitate her return to consciousness, Kate hastily untied the blood-soaked bandage and proceeded carefully to examine the wounded arm. "No bones broken, at any rate," she exclaimed with an air of satisfaction, raising her head for a moment and looking towards

Gilmour, who stood on the opposite side of the bed,
watching her absorbed face and unhesitating movements with a feeling of surprise and admiration.
" Will you please bring me that water ? " she said
next, pointing to a basin which stood in readiness
on a small table, together with a case of surgical
instruments and a roll of bandages. " If you can
move the table and all that is on it over here, so
much the better."

Gilmour lifted the table and brought it round to
where Kate stood, and then, in obedience to her
orders, held the basin for her while she carefully
washed the bleeding arm and adjusted the torn
parts.

By the time Kate had got the wound properly
bandaged, Ulu opened her eyes and looked round
her in dazed stupefaction at her unfamiliar surroundings. Slowly recognizing the friendly faces
bending over her, she sighed as if satisfied, and
wearily closed her eyes again.

" Take a little water, mtoto," said Kate, gently
passing her arm under Ulu's head, so as to raise
it a little. " There, do you feel better now ? " she
asked, as Ulu swallowed a mouthful from the glass
Kate held to her lips.

Ulu made no reply, but, with dumb, doglike
gratitude, wistfully raised her eyes to her bene-
factress's face, and looked from her to Gilmour and

back again, as if she did not know whom to thank, nor, indeed, how to thank them at all. Taking a pillow which Gilmour held in readiness, Kate bade the sufferer lie back on it, and once more gave her attention to the wounded arm. In the absence of proper splints, she adjusted it in a sling and pushed a pillow under the elbow to rest and steady it. That arrangement completed, Kate smoothed the coverlet, and, stooping down to pat Ulu softly on the head, laid strict injunctions on her patient to lie very still and try to go to sleep.

"Now, Uledi, it's time to attend to you," said Miss Kennedy, turning from the bedside as soon as she had seen Ulu comfortably settled. "I see you are bleeding too."

Gilmour turned quickly round. In his anxiety about Ulu, he had not noticed that his head-man's dress was torn at the shoulder, exposing to view some nasty scratches, from which blood was slowly trickling down the arm.

"Oh, bibi, it is nothing," cried Uledi, drawing back abashed at finding himself an object of so much solicitude.

"Better have it seen to, at any rate," replied Kate, practically. "Sit down, though," she added, pushing forward a chair; "I can't reach so high."

"Oh, Miss Kennedy, don't you trouble!" exclaimed Gimlour, assured from Uledi's expression that there was nothing seriously wrong. "I'll look after Uledi."

But Kate had already pushed aside the M-Swahili's torn dress, and was busy washing the blood from his wounds.

"I see it's nothing very serious," she said, pausing for a moment. "Just help me to adjust a bandage, Mr. Gilmour, please;" and Kate went on with her work in a matter-of-fact fashion, Gilmour lending her the desired assistance; while Ferhani looked on with wide-open eyes, and Uledi sat in mute wonderment at finding himself the object of such tender ministrations on the part of a bibi mzungu, whiter than the Bwana himself, and with hands so small and soft that to watch them at work was to forget the pain their gentle touch was bent on alleviating.

Just at the moment, perhaps, the embarrassment of the bibi's attentions was harder to bear than his physical pain, and, accordingly, it was with an air of intense relief that, when Kate had finished, he rose in obedience to her orders, and, along with Ferhani, shamefacedly left the room. When they had gone, Gilmour could not refrain from a teazing reference to Uledi's evident confusion, and the possible effect, not of music, but of medicine, as practised by lady doctors in soothing "the savage breast."

"Seems to me, I've done more towards raising a tumult than soothing him," answered Kate, smiling good-humouredly, and indicating the "savage" in question by a backward nod in the direction of the door by which he had departed. "I may console myself with the comforting reflection that it was 'for his good,' however," she continued, as she set to work to put the room to rights, noiselessly arranging the furniture and putting things back into their accustomed places.

"What can be keeping papa so long?" she exclaimed, as, order once more restored, she poured out some fresh water and began washing her hands. "He said he would go down to meet you. Did you not see him?"

"Yes; he met us at the gate and bade us come on here. He said he would follow us immediately. See, here he comes;" and Gilmour stopped to listen as a brisk step at that moment sounded in the porch.

"How goes the patient, Kate?" queried Mr. Kennedy, cheerfully, as he entered and crossed the room to where Ulu lay. "I met Uledi rejoicing in a proud display of bandage, and he told me the Bwana had said only Ulu's arm was hurt, and that the bibi had bound it up and put it to sleep on a pillow."

"You didn't think I had amputated it, papa,

did you ?" asked Kate, laughingly, as she dried her hands. "I was sorely tempted to try—just for the sake of practice, you know. But I was watched by a jealous eye, so I had to forego the luxury of an operation."

"You haven't answered my question yet, Kate," replied Mr. Kennedy, looking up from an anxious scrutiny of Ulu's pain-drawn lips and closed eyes ; "but I suppose you have made Ulu as comfortable as may be under the circumstances, or you wouldn't look so proud of yourself."

"Miss Kennedy has every reason to be proud of herself," put in Gilmour ; "she has done admirably in every way."

"Except in allowing so much talking in the sick-room," interrupted Kate, unwilling to stand and hear her own praises sounded. "Come, be off, both of you," she added, with pretended severity ; "my patient must have absolute quiet."

With a look of proud affection, Mr. Kennedy fondly kissed his daughter's cheek, and turned to re-enter the sitting-room, whither he was immediately followed by Gilmour, who felt rather worn out after the morning's excitement. In a few minutes they were joined by Kate, who noticed Gilmour's tired look, and asked if he would not like to lie down. Gilmour smiled at the typically feminine suggestion.

"Oh no, thank you," he said; "I shall do very well where I am."

"Well, we must have lunch a little earlier than usual. You look quite exhausted. I'll tell Ferjallah about it now. I'm going to get some milk for Ulu, at any rate;" and before Gilmour had time to remonstrate Kate was gone on her kindly errand.

Left alone with Gilmour, Mr. Kennedy very naturally began to make inquiries as to the particulars of Ulu's rescue, of which he had formed a not very clear idea from the confused and exaggerated accounts of the excited mission men. As briefly as might be, Gilmour told the story, not without some rather severe strictures on the cowardly conduct of the Pisgahites, whose untimely flight had nearly led to such disastrous consequences. Mr. Kennedy listened attentively, almost without comment, and for some time after Gilmour had ceased speaking, he remained silent, apparently lost in thought. It was not encouraging to hear that his people had acquitted themselves so discreditably.

"It is strange," he said at length, "how even the Christian religion has failed to imbue those men with moral force sufficient to overcome the purely animal instinct of self-preservation."

"I think it is scarcely to be wondered at when one considers their so very nearly animal brain."

The missionary winced. This was a way of stating the case he did not much like.

"You don't take a very hopeful view of our negro brother," he said, after a brief pause. "Has closer acquaintance not convinced you of his capacity for a higher and more enlightened life? What about Ulu, by-the-by?" he exclaimed with sudden animation, rousing himself from his pensive attitude, and drawing his chair closer to Gilmour's. "How do you reconcile your low opinion of the capabilities of the savage nature with your intention of marrying her?"

"I do not attempt to reconcile them. I recognize too clearly the impossibility of making Ulu other than she is, an out-and-out little savage, childlike and simple, and lovable in many ways, perhaps, but utterly incapable of assimilating any of the higher thoughts and aspirations of the civilized life."

"Ah, Mr. Gilmour, it is because you begin at the wrong end," said Mr. Kennedy, earnestly. "You set to work from without inwards instead of from within outwards. First touch the heart with a live coal from the Lord's altar, and, its deceit and wickedness consumed, the outer life will soon become pure and holy."

"The difficulty is how to touch the heart. You can't reach it except through the brain, just as you can't reach the brain except through the ear or the eye. You *must* begin at the outside."

"But Christianity appeals directly to the heart."

"Only through the understanding; and how is the low, stunted brain of the negro capable of comprehending and assimilating the high and complex system of Christian morality, the slowly evolved product of centuries of divine precept made visible in human practice? It took two thousand years of obedience to moral precept—a palpable 'thou shalt' and 'thou shalt not'—before the world was ready for the new and higher revelation. It has taken nearly two thousand years more of gradual mental and moral evolution for that revelation to become, even nominally, the acknowledged principle underlying Western civilization. By what miracle is it possible—how can any one expect, in the course of a few months or years, or even of a whole lifetime, out of the lowest animalism and barbarism, to produce the highest purity and spirituality?"

"'With God all things are possible,'" quoted Mr. Kennedy reverently. "We do not enter on the work in our own strength, else we should speedily be crushed beneath the sense of its magnitude and of our own littleness. God has sent us into His vineyard. It is for Paul to plant, for

Apollos to water. In His own good time God will give the increase."

Gilmour shrugged his shoulders. " I suppose it is scarcely possible for you and me to look at these things with the same eyes, Mr. Kennedy," he said. " To my mind the soil still wants a vast amount of preparation before it can be ready for either planting or watering. Of God the negro has but the very crudest conception ; of morality absolutely none. To develop the one and create the other is as much as any religion need attempt in the mean time. See what a vast influence for good Mohammedanism is proving in Africa, simply because it does not attempt too much. A clear and constant iteration of the existence of one God, a few simple rules for the guidance of conduct in this life, with the assurance, according as these are kept or broken, of a place in a very real heaven or a very real hell in the next—these sum up the teaching of Mahomet, and constitute a religious system, the highest, it would seem, which the negro mind is at present capable of grasping."

" And you would say it's no good trying to teach Christianity because it includes something higher and more abstract, and is therefore less easy of comprehension ? " said Mr. Kennedy, looking as if he thought Gilmour's cool way of discussing the relative merits of the Christian and the Mohammedan religion as something little short of blasphemy.

"Yes," returned Gilmour; "just as I would say it's no good trying to teach the differential calculus to a child who doesn't know simple arithmetic. We must progress step by step."

"What's that you were saying about the 'differential calculus,' Mr. Gilmour?" asked Kate, who had returned unobserved, just in time to catch a word or two of Gilmour's last remark. "You're not worrying papa with mathematics, are you?" she went on cheerily, dimly conscious of an atmosphere of trouble between the two men, and good-naturedly wishful to dissipate it. "The science has been his pet antipathy ever since his juvenile failure to cross the 'asses' bridge' at one step."

Mr. Kennedy smiled absently. Gilmour looked up and smiled too.

"No," he said, with an apologetic look towards his host. "I'm afraid I have 'worried' Mr. Kennedy about something that affects him more deeply than mathematics. We were talking of the possibility of elevating the negro. The conversation arose, I think, out of something your father asked me about Ulu."

"Did you tell papa you wanted us to have her here for a time?" interrupted Kate, eagerly, as Gilmour hesitated and tried to recall what had passed.

"Wanted us to have her here!" cried Mr. Kennedy, suddenly startled out of the painful reverie into which he seemed to have fallen. "Why, Mr. Gilmour, after what you have just said, how can you expect me to succeed where you have failed?"

Gilmour looked rather abashed. "It wasn't so much that," he said slowly. "I thought Miss Kennedy, being a woman, would know better how to reach her than I. Besides, as I have already explained to Miss Kennedy, the women at Pepo-ni are jealous of Ulu."

"Yes, papa," said Kate, taking up the tale; "and they make it very hot for the poor little thing. And, of course, in a little place like Pepo-ni, Mr. Gilmour can't very well keep her out of their way, and—— Oh, there are ever so many things to make the situation extremely awkward both for Mr. Gilmour and for Ulu, don't you see?" she concluded, rather vaguely, but none the less sympathetically, her woman's instinct having guessed how very much more "awkward" the situation might be than Gilmour could explain to her.

Mr. Kennedy still looked dubious. He could not all at once reconcile the wish to place Ulu under his care, which to him meant simply to bring her within the sphere of Christian influence, with

Gilmour's recently expressed opinion of the futility
of that influence to effect any deep and lasting
change in negro life and conduct. For a moment
he almost felt inclined once more to doubt the
integrity of the young man's intentions towards
the M-Chaga maiden; but he had only to recollect
Gilmour's honest, downright way of looking at
things, his direct, almost blunt, manner of speech,
to feel convinced that, whatever he was in religion,
he was in morals above suspicion. A time had
been when any one expressing the opinions Gilmour had maintained in their recent conversation
would have stood condemned as capable of every
form of wickedness. Under his daughter's influence, however, the missionary's views had lately
undergone considerable modification. From contact with her, and from the effort to appreciate the
standpoint from which she viewed the world and
life in general, he had come to realize that, though
for him the world had practically stood still for
more than twenty years, it had not done so for
others; that there were new ideas current in
society and new forces at work, which had revo-
lutionized thought, and, if they had made men less
full of unquestioning faith, had given them more
independence and more earnestness in the search
for truth, and more discontent with all that comes
short of it. Still, as regards Gilmour, there was

much that needed explanation. If the young man had such an eye for the detection of social shams—as Mr. Kennedy believed he had, judging from remarks he had passed at various times—why had he not stayed to do his best to eradicate them? Then, since he had, for some unknown reason, chosen to make his home in Africa, why had he for so long remained passive, making no effort for either the spiritual or physical welfare of the natives? Above all, why, now that he had begun to do something for at least one individual—why did he want to shift the burden of the responsibilities he had undertaken to other shoulders than his own? Had it been only a whim, and had he tired of it? Had he tired of Africa, too, and was he perhaps meditating a speedy return to Europe? Had he——

" Don't you think it would be for Ulu's good as well as for her comfort," urged Kate, breaking in upon her father's speculations at this point, and passing round to the back of his chair to seat herself on its arm, to be within better " coaxing distance," as she was wont to put it.

" But—— " began Mr. Kennedy.

" Oh, blessed ' but,' herald of joyous ' yes! ' " exclaimed Kate, interrupting him, and laying her hand caressingly on his shoulder. " Now, daddy dear, do just say ' yes ' at once."

"Well, then, 'yes,' provided Ulu would like to remain."

"Oh, but Ulu must remain—at least, in the mean time. She's a close prisoner here for ten days, at the very least. After that——"

"After that," continued Gilmour, "you must all come down to Pepo-ni to compare notes and make final arrangements. Perhaps it will be better, in any case, for Mr. Kennedy not to decide until he has thought the matter over."

"All right, then," said Kate; "talk it over between you. I must be off now to look after my patient;" and she slipped from her uneasy seat and disappeared into the sick-room.

One important result of the conversation which ensued between Mr. Kennedy and Gilmour was to bring about in each a better understanding and appreciation of the other's character and modes of thought. Without alluding to the causes which had led him to seek the wild seclusion of Kilimanjaro, Gilmour spoke frankly of the despondent and dissatisfied mood in which Seri's proposition that he should marry Ulu had come to him, and of the specious reasoning by which he had deluded himself into the belief that it was possible for him seriously to entertain it. He told how gradually and unwillingly the opposite conclusion had forced itself upon him, as he saw how useless it was to

hope in such a marriage for even an approximation
to that companionship of soul which can alone
constitute any true union. He explained in detail
how the conduct of his women had rendered it
imperative either that he should marry Ulu or find
a home for her that would in some sort resemble
his own, since, having accustomed her to easier
and gentler conditions of life, he could not allow
her to return to the slavery and degradation which
is the accustomed lot of the ordinary M-Chaga
woman. He no longer pretended, as he had done
to Kate, that he still intended to fulfil his romantic
purpose, though, of course, he did not tell—he
scarcely yet acknowledged to himself—how much
the dissipation of his daydream had been hastened
by his meeting with Miss Kennedy and the renewed
hold which, through her, the civilized social life
seemed to have gained upon his imagination.

Mr. Kennedy, however, though he did not suspect
the cause, was shrewd enough to guess, from the
fact that Gilmour no longer inveighed so vehemently
against civilization, and no longer desired to link
himself indissolubly with its opposite, that there
had been some new birth of hope and purpose in
the young man's mind. That in itself was enough
to lead him to listen attentively to all Gilmour had
to say, and to repress much of the question and
criticism that instinctively rose to his lips. Active

and practical, the missionary had but little sympathy with morbid moods that led to months of
wasted life; but, earnestly as he desired to see
Gilmour assume the *rôle* of a worker in the world,
he had tact enough to know that to advise or
exhort at the present critical juncture would only
be to call forth on Gilmour's part an obstinate
defence of the attitude of apathy he had chosen to
assume. He saw that Gilmour was passing through
some great mental and moral crisis, and he believed
that the best thing he could do was to let him
speak freely whatever came into his mind, hoping
at some future time to be able to give such counsel
as God might put it into his heart to offer.

Accordingly, Gilmour's confidences, if such they
might be called, were received with unlooked-for
tolerance and interest; and when, in the afternoon,
our hero set out to return to Pepo-ni, he was surprised to find himself taking leave of the missionary
with something very like regret. Both Mr. Kennedy and Kate were most pressing in their invita-
tion to him to stay longer; but he declined to
trespass further on their kindness, fearing that,
with Ulu an invalid and Miss Kennedy evidently
bent on nursing her as tenderly as if she had been
a sister, his presence in the house might only
prove an additional source of trouble. Kate under-
took to let him know from time to time how her

little charge progressed; and, with a promise on his part to come again soon and see them all, Gilmour bade his hospitable friends good-bye, and started on his way homewards.

CHAPTER III.

Gilmour had closed the idyl of Pepo-ni. In committing Ulu to the care of Miss Kennedy, he felt that he had severed the one golden thread which had become interwoven with the dreary dullness of his life of exile. In the days which succeeded his visit to Pisgah, he was surprised to find what a strange blank the mtoto's absence left unfilled. True, he no longer deceived himself as to the nature of the bond which had united them. Ulu had been to him "a little dearer than his dog"— no more; but for a time, at least, he had been able to toy with the idea that she might become more, and the specious fancy had shed a halo over his futile attempts to draw out the deeper nature which as a human being he had supposed she must possess. She had been a curious study to him. He had found much food for thought in noting her various moods, her simple method of looking at things, her artless way of explaining the forces which she saw in operation around her.

Still more had Gilmour been interested in observing the manifestations of his little pupil's purely animal nature, the utter absence of any higher or more spiritual promptings beyond those springing from mere family relationships. What a contrast between her and the "white maiden of Mandara's"—the one, with her low appetites and passions, finding her paradise in plenty of food, gaudy clothes, and idleness; the other, with her noble aspirations "for the pure and the true, and the beauteous and the right," dreaming only of satisfaction in constant activity and earnest endeavour for the welfare of humanity. Strange that such opposite forces should have influenced him to such similar purpose—both urging him back to his place in the world, the one by the despair she had finally intensified, the other by the hope she had unconsciously awakened. Deprived of either, what would Gilmour by this time have become? Ulu had first supplied an object in his aimless life; had drawn him out of himself, and away from his persistent, morbid contemplation of the more artificial and disappointing aspects of human nature. While yet under the inspiration of his fresh effort and sanguine of its success, Miss Kennedy had appeared on the scene, soon to become an important factor in the working out of his spiritual regeneration—all the more important that his effort had ended in comparative failure.

To Gilmour Kate was Europe personified. She embodied all that was best and sweetest and fairest of its ardent youthful thought and active spirit. In everything she said or did, or even looked, she recalled to him the charm of the old life and the freshness of his early hopes; it seemed, indeed, as if she had been specially sent to Kilimanjaro to remind him how much of goodness and truth and beauty still leavened the great body of humanity, and prevented it from becoming an altogether stale, sodden, unprofitable mass. Kate's eager enthusiasm, her faith in man, her impulsive, un-calculating manner of speaking out whatever thought originated in her heart—all found a responsive echo in Gilmour's own nature, and told him that the old, impetuous, sanguine self was only dormant and not dead, as he had fondly endeavoured to persuade himself. Whenever in Kate's presence he had tried to maintain his assumed attitude of cynical pessimism, and she, in her direct way of looking at people, had bent her candid, heart-searching eyes upon him, as if she would read his inmost soul, he had been conscious of an uneasy conviction that she saw through his affectation; and even if she in some sort sympathized with the despondency of which it had been the outcome, she was none the less ready to condemn the idle, contemptible life in which it had resulted. The suggestion of latent energy—of will and capacity to do—which seemed to emanate from her whole mental and physical bearing, was in itself a rebuke to inaction; and her spoken conviction of the duty of work, and of its efficacy as a remedy for spiritual distemper, Gilmour had recognized and acknowledged as a direct appeal to him to rouse himself from his lethargy, and once more join issue on the side of right and progress.

Many a lonely hour Gilmour spent musing on his strange experiences of the past few weeks, and, what was better, dimly forming plans for the guidance of his future. More and more his thoughts tended towards Europe, his first half-formed, hastily suppressed desire turning to persistent yearning. He felt as if now he could approach life with a clearer and more matured conception of the possibilities it contained, with more reasonable expectations, and a humbler and truer estimate of his own rights and his own powers. He would do more and dream less, and, because not attempting too much, might possibly achieve more practical results. Already he saw himself launched forth on the old strife, better equipped for the rude tussle with the world, and better fitted to do something which, in however minute a way, would help to benefit his fellows, and contribute towards the upward tendency of humanity.

It was not without much hesitation and regret that Gilmour finally made up his mind to quit Africa for home. In doing so, there would be much left behind that he had become attached to—his charming model settlement, his faithful followers, his little savage pupil—all these had become part of his daily life, and could not be taken leave of without a pang. More than all, perhaps, he felt he would regret breaking off the intimacy with Miss Kennedy, for whom a strong feeling of friendship had sprung up within him. They had found so much essentially in common between them; while their surface differences seemed only to form the complement one of the other, and became, therefore, bonds of union rather than points of separation.

Without the slightest vanity, Gilmour felt, too, that Miss Kennedy would miss him almost more than he would miss her. With her yearning for the civilized life, her want of enthusiasm for the work in which her father, and in a sense she herself, was engaged; with no one at hand to whom she could freely unburden her soul, no friend with whom to exchange thoughts, nothing but a few books to link her mind with the enlightened world which had her heart—would she not slowly wear out all the fire and vivacity of her nature, chafing at her uncongenial environment? Much as she loved her father, there were too many subjects on which there was a tacit understanding of silence between them for her ever to feel that his companionship atoned for the want of all other society. The missionary's life had been too isolated, his thoughts too much concentrated on a single object, for him to have much sympathy with many of the aspects of his daughter's many-sided character. Much that burned within her for expression must thus of necessity smoulder as a secret fire, and, finding no natural outlet, would prey upon her inner life with, it might be, disastrous results.

Gilmour had not failed to remark how eager Kate was to talk with him, and with what pleasure she threw herself into the discussion of her favourite themes, her ardour sometimes causing her to launch forth at great, and what to many might have seemed tedious, length, though Gilmour had no fault to find with it. She expressed herself so clearly; her thoughts, it seemed to him, were in themselves so well worth hearing, and her enthusiasm and fire so delightfully refreshing and invigorating, that, as he listened, he caught the infection of her mood, and, far from feeling tired, took pleasure in inciting her to go on.

Perhaps it was purely out of consideration for Miss Kennedy, perhaps because he still felt unable to decide exactly *when* he would return to Europe, perhaps from some reason altogether more subtle and indefinable, that during the fortnight or more Ulu remained at Pisgah as an invalid, Gilmour did not once go to see her. Messengers frequently passed between Pepo-ni and the mission settlement, and more than once Gilmour sent flowers— rare and splendid blossoms from high up the mountain-side, such as had seemed to afford Kate such intense pleasure on that day when he had first seen her in her own home. Still Gilmour did not go himself, a circumstance at which Kate wondered not a little, especially after his parting promise to come again soon.

Kate did not resent Gilmour's non-appearance, however. He was her friend, and all Kate's friends she was inclined to view through rose-coloured spectacles. She knew, moreover, that Gilmour was in a state of mental unrest and indecision that excused unexpected actions, and demanded patience and toleration on the part of those about him. As day after day went by, she became more and more certain that he was struggling towards some important turning-point in his career, and in the satisfaction she derived from the idea, she was content to be without the pleasure of his society until such time as he himself should feel in the mood for hers.

Meanwhile, happy in the consciousness of having

a kindred spirit near her, Kate went about her
daily duties with more of interest than she had
ever before been able to take in things African, and
ceaselessly busied herself about Ulu, for whose
welfare—physical, mental, and moral—she now
felt herself to be responsible.

Miss Kennedy's painstaking kindness did not go
unrewarded. In the depths of Ulu's rude nature
there gradually grew up a deep devotion for her
untiring nurse and teacher.

The bibi's tender care, her soothing touch when
dressing her wounds, were a constant source of
wonder to Ulu. It seemed incredible that a being
so exalted, so rich, so beautiful, should care to
trouble herself about a poor little mshenzi. Vainly
she strove to find an explanation of her difficulty,
believing at first that under all the attention Kate
lavished upon her there must be an interested
motive, and that the time would come when she
would rue the hour in which she had fallen into
the bibi's hands. But day after day passed by,
and still the bibi looked upon her with the same
tender eye, still dressed her wounds with the same
gentle care, as if she—Ulu, the M-Chaga maiden—
were a queen and the bibi her slave.

Ulu gained confidence. After all, there was to
be no rude awakening, no evil outcome of the
present incomprehensible good. The bibi was a

ministering spirit—Ngai (God) Himself perhaps; that was the conclusion to which Ulu was forced to come, and in her heart she worshipped Kate accordingly, with a mixture of love, fear, and awe, which robbed her of words, and found expression in her great gazelle-like eyes and timid, submissive manner.

In thus reverencing Kate as a deity, Ulu was, as already hinted, by no means singular. More or less the bibi mzungu was regarded in that light throughout the length and breadth of Kindi, as much from the idea of mystery and superiority with which she impressed the native mind, as from her kindness and success in treating disease.

At first the M-Chaga had looked upon Gilmour, too, in much the same aspect; but his disgust at the civilization from which he had fled led him to adapt himself in more rough and ready fashion to the rude life around him, while his good-natured hab.t of conversing with the natives, as if one of themselves, soon served to dispel the primary awe and fear his appearance had occasioned. Though familiarity by no means bred contempt, it yet reduced him to a much lower pedestal than that on which the simple people had naturally been inclined to place him.

With Kate, however, it was different. She had no fault to find with civilization, and, bound up as

she was in all that pertained to the civilized social
life, Kate Kennedy on Kilimanjaro was the same
Kate who had been the presiding genius of the
student circle in Edinburgh. Without consciously
intending to hold herself aloof, she yet made little
or no attempt to get *en rapport* with the natives, as
Gilmour had done ; and thus, isolated and alone,
she moved a goddess among thousands, with kind
words, it is true, and speech adapted to their comprehension, but always Kate Kennedy, always the
being whose thoughts were not their thoughts,
though herself in kind akin.

Never before had Kate been brought into such
intimate contact with a native as she now was
with Ulu, and for some time she was at a loss to
explain the girl's timid attitude towards her. She
had, she thought, done everything in her power to
gain the love and confidence of her little charge,
and it was disappointing to find that, spite of all
her efforts, Ulu still seemed half afraid to approach
or speak to her. It was only by accident that she
at length discovered the key to the mystery.

One day, by the hand of Uledi, Gilmour sent
Kate a magnificent bouquet of orchids, some of
which were so rare and so exquisite that she took
a fancy to perpetuate their loveliness on canvas.
She was just putting the finishing touches to her
study, when Ulu, by this time almost well, stole

softly behind her chair, and stood silently watching her movements with admiring, wonder-stricken eyes.

"Bibi, do you go in the night to Pepo-ni?" questioned the little maid at length, her voice lowered to a whisper.

Kate stopped her painting and looked round. What could Ulu mean by such a question as that? "What did you say, mtoto?" she asked, thinking she had not heard aright. "Do I go in the night to Pepo-ni?"

"I never saw you; it must have been in the night," said Ulu, hesitatingly, mistaking Kate's look of bewilderment for one of displeasure. "Oh, bibi, next time you go, will you take me with you?" she timidly entreated. "I want so much to see the Bwana again."

More and more puzzled, and vexed by the child's half-frightened manner, Kate put her arm encouragingly around her.

"Of course," she said, in answer to Ulu's request; "but we can't go for a day or two yet. You are not strong enough to walk so far."

"But the flowers will die," objected Ulu, doubtfully.

"Well, what if they do? We're not going to take them with us."

"Where will you take them, then? Will you plant them on the mountain?"

"No, of course not. I shall put them in my own room. That was what the Bwana sent them for."

For a moment there was silence, during which Kate sat wondering what was to be the outcome of all this question and answer; for, from Ulu's doubtful expression, she inferred they were still at cross-purposes.

"Why does the Bwana send you flowers?" asked Ulu at length, gazing inquiringly into Kate's face.

"I don't know. I suppose because he thinks I like them."

"And when did you give them to him? Did you take them yourself?"

"Ulu, what *do* you mean?" cried Kate, unable to repress a smile at the evident misunderstanding, which seemed never going to be cleared up. "You know it was the Bwana who gave them to me."

"But you gave them to him first. You put them where he could find them. You made them for him."

"I? I cannot make flowers."

It was now Ulu's turn to look bewildered. "But I have seen you," she said confidently. "I saw you just now;" and Ulu pointed to the canvas on the easel before her.

Kate saw at once what she was thinking. To Ulu the painted flowers were real.

" Never had such a compliment to my artistic efforts before ! " was Kate's mental ejaculation. Aloud she said, smiling, " Ah, mtoto, I'm afraid you won't find my flowers nearly so nice as the Bwana's. You can't pluck them, nor smell them. See, if you only do that, they are gone ; " and Kate drew Ulu's forefinger across the wet canvas, and remorselessly smudged out part of her carefully finished work.

Ulu gazed at her aghast ; she seemed more dumfoundered than ever. " But the malaam told me you could make flowers," she stammered forth, after standing for a moment looking from Kate to the picture, and from the picture to her own paint-smeared finger, and from the finger back again to Kate's amused face.

" Oh no, Ulu ; the malaam could not tell you that," cried Kate, wondering what fresh revelation was in store for her.

" Yes, he did," returned Ulu, with assurance ; " he told me Ngai (God) made everything—the flowers, the—— "

" Ngai ! " repeated Kate, in blank astonishment, scarcely able to believe her ears.

Did Ulu think that *she* was Ngai ? This, then, was the explanation of the child's incomprehensible

timidity in approaching her; of the awe and sub-
mission with which she obeyed Kate's smallest
behest, and listened to her lightest word.   It
seemed strange Kate had not thought of it before;
but, as she told her father when relating the little
episode at dinner that evening, she had become so
accustomed to regard Ulu in the light of her intimate connection with Gilmour, that she could
never class her with the other natives, as one
absolutely ignorant of even the primary conceptions
of a civilized religion.

As best she might, Kate set about trying to alter
the erroneous idea Ulu had formed regarding her.
The task was by no means easy.   When Kate
spoke of her own limited capacity, and in a simple
way tried to teach Ulu something of the nature
and attributes of deity, the girl only looked at her
with troubled eyes that spoke her perplexity of
soul, and plainly showed Kate's efforts were futile.

Ulu's idea of a God was vague and undefined;
anything wonderful and incomprehensible was to
her divine.   Kate, in act and aspect, was *the* most
wonderful being she had known, and seemed to
realize the most wonderful she was capable of
conceiving.   She was more than content with this
visible embodiment of power and beneficence, and
it seemed superfluous to try to substitute for it an
invisible spirit, who might be everywhere, as the

bibi said, but, as always unseen, appeared to be nowhere.

Ulu had no words in which to express her feelings on the subject—nay, could not well define them to herself; but, after a fashion, Kate guessed the tendency of the girl's dim thoughts, and sympathized with it. For the present, therefore, she gave up trying to force upon Ulu's darkened mind an idea it was incapable of grasping; but during the next few days she spoke much to her of the God of the mzungu, and was rewarded at length by finding that her little pupil had gained the idea of a Being who was to the bibi what the bibi was to her, though she did not on that account think the bibi any less worthy her reverence and devotion. It was not much, but it was better than nothing; and in the mean time Kate had to be content, and await with what patience she might the development of that "little soul," in whose progress she now felt as deep an interest as had at one time Gilmour himself.

CHAPTER IV.

ON a warm afternoon, rather more than a fortnight after his visit to the mission settlement, Gilmour, arrayed in all the glory of a spotless drill suit and crimson silk neckerchief, was restlessly pacing up and down his baraza at Pepo-ni, awaiting with impatience the arrival of Miss Kennedy and her father, who on that day were to come on a short visit to Pepo-ni. Ulu was to accompany them; and Gilmour hoped that now final arrangements might be made for his little mtoto's permanent residence at Pisgah.

As he listened anxiously for the first signal of the approach of his guests, Gilmour turned over in his mind how he would tell Miss Kennedy of his intended departure for Europe, and pictured to himself the mingled expression that would pass over Kate's speaking face on hearing the news— approbation of the step he was about to take, glad- ness at the change of mental attitude it indicated, regret for the loss of her newly made friend, her only friend within thousands of miles.

"Dear me!" he exclaimed at length, "they should be here by this time."

Looking out, he remarked that the sun was within an hour of the zenith. With a gesture of surprise, he was about to cross the compound to the gate, when he suddenly stopped short in an attitude of rapt attention. With body bent forward and head slightly turned to one side, he presented his ear towards the west.

Away in the far distance, a strange sound could be faintly heard, ringing with a peculiar intonation, which brought a look of intense anxiety to Gilmour's face. Quickly the sound grew and gathered force, taken up by an ever-increasing number of voices, till it seemed to emanate from all directions at once.

Onward, with astounding rapidity and ever-increasing volume and area, the dread note which betokens war came rolling towards Pepo-ni, passed above and below it, and continued its startling progress towards Machamé and western Chaga. Not a soul was to be seen, though in front and rear, to the right and to the left, the cry was taken up with deafening clamour, till the little settlement seemed the centre of some vast battle-field.

The word which went most directly to the hearts

of those who heard was one which served to indicate the nature of the danger. " El-Masai! El-
Masai! " was the name which rang out upon the
startled air, with paralyzing effect.

No one stood more spellbound than Gilmour on
hearing that cry of bloody import. His friends,
the Kennedys—where were they? Something must
at once be done to save them, if, indeed, it were
not already too late.

"Bunduki, bunduki!" (guns, guns) he cried to
his men, who stood expectantly, awaiting his
orders.

"Tayari, tayari!" (ready, ready) was the reply,
as, with convulsive grasp, the Wa-Swahili shook
their weapons in the air like spears; while the
women shrank back in terror, and their children
cowered beside them, clutching at their mothers'
garments with nervous little hands.

Meanwhile, Tubu, divining the requirements of
the situation, had brought his master's rifle and
belt. Hastily Gilmour buckled on the latter, and
seized his gun.

"Now, then, boys, come along. There's no
time to be lost;" and swiftly Gilmour led the way
to the gate.

"Eh-wallah!" shouted the men, following him
pellmell.

Once outside the stockade, they fell into single

file, and, headed by Gilmour, rapidly traversed the outer bush tract. Soon they emerged upon more open ground, where they were able to proceed more freely.

Everywhere they encountered numbers of men hurrying to join the fighters at Seri's, and others flying, like cowards, to hide themselves in the bush, or take refuge at Pepo-ni. More slowly came groups of terrified women, every moment expecting a Masai spear through their backs, or the crash of a knobkerry on their skulls. But maternal instincts rose superior to every fear, every danger, and babes were clasped convulsively to breast, an aiding hand held out to children, as one and all they toiled gaspingly up the hill.

Of every one Gilmour asked, "Where are the Masai? Are there many? Have you seen the white people of Mandara's?" but only senseless cries were elicited in answer. His impotency made him frantic. He knew not where to go or what to do. There were several roads by which his friends might come. He stopped to take counsel of his men. All showed themselves eager to return.

"What can *we* do against the Masai?" they asked.

What, indeed, could they do? was Gilmour's own despairing question. And yet—the Kennedys! —Gilmour could not desert them without doing his

utmost, whatever might be the risk. He was just
on the point of going forward again on chance,
when one of his men attracted his attention to a
flying figure appearing - and disappearing among
the bushes.

"Look, Bwana! there is the mzungu," he cried.

With an exclamation of delight, Gilmour started
in pursuit. Soon it was seen that the man was
only one of Mr. Kennedy's servants.

"Ngoja! ngoja!" (stop) shouted Gilmour, some
of his men joining in the cry.

The fugitive only redoubled his speed. It was
evident, however, that he was rapidly becoming
exhausted; whereupon Ferhani forged ahead, and
seized the coat-tails of Jonathan Uledi. With a
wild scream of terror, the M-Chaga collapsed helplessly on the pathway, pulling Ferhani over on the
top of him.

"Lord, have mercy upon me! Lord, have mercy
upon me!" he kept calling, as he lay face down-
wards on the ground.

"Kelélé, mjenga!" (silence, fool) cried Gilmour,
who arrived panting. "We are not Masai," he
continued in English, giving the fellow a shake.

Immediately Jonathan's clamour ceased, and,
scarcely daring to trust his senses, he raised his
head and took a timid glance at his captors. On
seeing the white man, the revulsion of feeling was

so great that he could only clasp Gilmour's knees
and blubber and laugh hysterically.

Gilmour shook him off. " Tell me what has
come over your master and mistress," he said
impatiently.

Jonathan found his tongue at once. "Oh,
Bwana, Bwana, they are all killed," he stammered
out—"all killed by the Masai;" and once more he
betook himself to his childish wailing, rocking himself to and fro the while.

For a moment Gilmour was too much agitated
to speak. "Who are killed?" he asked at length,
in a choking tone. "Not the Bwana and Bibi
Kennedy?"

"Yes, yes; they are murdered. The Masai have
murdered them," groaned Jonathan, with another
outburst of lamentation.

Gilmour stared at the man helplessly. Mechanically he asked where the tragedy took place.

"Quite near," sobbed Jonathan.

"Were the Masai numerous?"

"Oh, Bwana, numerous as the ants;" and
Jonathan, reminded of the dangers of his situation,
jumped hastily to his feet, and would once more
have taken flight, had not Gilmour laid a restraining hand upon him.

"Not so fast, my man," he said; "you must
show us the place."

A cry of remonstrance broke from some of his followers.

"What!" he continued, turning fiercely upon them, "have I cowards among my watoto?"

The stinging epithet had its due effect.

"We will follow you to death!" shouted some one more brave than the rest.

"Lead on, Bwana; our lives are in your hand," chimed in some of the others, becoming emboldened.

"Ngemma! now I recognize my men. You would not leave my friends a prey to the hyænas and vultures?"

"No, no! Let us go to them at once," cried one and all, inspired by their master's fire.

"Now, then, Jonathan, show the way;" and Gilmour grasped his rifle more firmly, as if to prepare for whatever dangers might be in front of him.

Keeping carefully in the depths of the wood, lest any of the Masai should still be prowling about, the little party soon reached the spot where the attack had taken place. The first object which greeted them was the frightfully gashed body of Kennedy's donkey boy. Gilmour dared scarcely look further. Every moment he expected to come upon the mutilated corpse of the missionary or his daughter. His men scattered to examine the bushes, but for some time their search was fruitless. Gilmour began faintly to hope that, after all, his friends might have effected their escape. He was just about to ask Jonathan if he had seen his master killed, when an excited shout froze the words upon his lips.

"Bwana, Bwana," cried the men, eagerly crowding around some object on the ground, "here is the malaam!"

Quick as thought Gilmour sprang to the place. There, indeed, lay the missionary, without a sign of life, a stream of blood slowly oozing from a ghastly wound in his side. Mr. Kennedy had crept into the bush to die.

"Has no one seen the bibi?" asked Gilmour, as he turned sadly away.

An expressive silence was his only answer.

Again the men scattered and resumed their search. In vain; not a trace of Miss Kennedy or Ulu was to be found. The thought occurred to Gilmour that they might have been made prisoners. Ere he had time to utter it, a cry, with a curious, unfamiliar ring about it, came wafted to his ears. He looked inquiringly at Uledi, his usual oracle.

"El-Masai," was the brief response.

A new idea crossed Gilmour's mind. He might yet make sure whether Kate was a prisoner or not. With quick decision, he gave his orders. So many of his men were to make a litter and carry the body of the missionary to Pepo-ni, while so many more were to remain in the wood and continue the search for Miss Kennedy. These arrangements completed, he and Uledi hurried off in a south-westerly direction at break-neck speed. In a quarter of an hour they reached the base of a steep, parasitic, volcanic cone, which rose at the base of the mountain, and commanded a clear view of the Kahé plain. Soon they were at the top, and before them lay an open grassy glade, which here extended through the forest, as if artificially cleared. Panting, master and man threw themselves flat on the ground, and with feverish expectancy watched for the passage of the savages. For some time it seemed as if they were doomed to be disappointed. At length one dark figure appeared from the forest, then another and another, until by-and-by a file of warriors, dressed in all the awe-inspiring fierceness of war-array, stretched across the entire width of the clearing. Still there was no sign of Kate.

Next a herd of cattle—part of the spoil of the raid—appeared, guarded on all sides by agile spearmen. That passed, and became lost to view. The procession seemed to have ended; and Gilmour's heart sank, as, full of dire forebodings, he anxiously asked himself what could have become of Miss Kennedy. But again the stream of savages

commenced. Something white showed itself among
the trees, and the next moment Gilmour saw Miss
Kennedy's donkey, Tanga, step into the clearing,
bearing on its back the object of his solicitude.
Kate looked dazed and stupefied ; grief and terror
had almost bereft her of her senses. One warrior
led the donkey; while half a dozen others surrounded the captive, their swarthy figures throwing
her white dress into more marked relief.

The one feeling which overwhelmed Gilmour at
the sight was relief to find Miss Kennedy still
alive. Then he remembered his impotency to help
her. He felt a mad desire to shoot some of her
captors down ; but he restrained himself, and
gazed on in a stupor.

"Look, Bwana, there is Ulu ! " cried Uledi.

True enough, there was the little M-Chaga, jogging
along patiently behind Tanga. Gilmour was pleased
to observe that she, too, was safe for the moment,
and thought with satisfaction that probably she
would be able to make herself of use to Kate in her
present straits.

The little group had now reached the middle of
the clearing. A few minutes more, and Kate would
be hid from Gilmour's eyes, perhaps for ever. He
sprang to his feet, determined to signal to her as a
token that her position was known, and that she
was not deserted. He fired his gun. As the sharp

crack re-echoed on every hand, a great commotion ensued, the Masai thinking they were about to be attacked. Kate was the centre around which they rallied, and in a twinkling she was hemmed in by a hundred warriors, eager to meet the expected enemy.

Again Gilmour fired. All eyes were turned towards the hill, and a wild yell rang out, as the white dress of the white man was easily discerned. A hundred shovel-headed spears flashed in the air, ready to do their bloody office. For a moment Kate was hid from view; but Gilmour knew that her eyes would be directed towards him, as to her only hope. Tying his handkerchief to his rifle, he waved it high above his head. He caught a glimpse of a responsive wave of something white. That was enough; it was time now to fly. A dozen warriors had stealthily detached themselves from the rest, and started in pursuit of him. One last wave of his handkerchief, one last look at the figure in the white dress, and Gilmour and Uledi disappeared down the hill.

CHAPTER V.

MISS KENNEDY was very bright and radiant on that
August morning when she started with Ulu for
Pepo-ni. She was looking forward eagerly to the
prospect of another long talk with Gilmour, whom
she had much to tell of her experiences with his
ex-pupil. She hoped, too, that Gilmour would
now tell her something about himself. Her
curiosity was piqued by the mystery which surrounded him; she felt as if she would like to know
what the "environment" had been that had produced her new friend's mood of artificial cynicism,
and the sensitive, romantic soul which underlay it.
She felt, too, as if she would like to help towards
his conversion back to saner and less bitter ideas.
The task was one which suited her better than
the ineffectual endeavour to get in touch with the
low minds of the Wa-Chaga. She wondered if
he had ever thought any more of their last conversation, wondered if the words which had then

so much moved him had had any lasting effect. Somehow Kate was inclined to answer in the affirmative, and perhaps there was not wanting a tiny spice of feminine vanity in the pleasure the thought gave her that she had been able to influence Gilmour for good.

Mr. Kennedy was not less anxious than his daughter to see Mr. Gilmour again. His darling project of founding a station at Seri's was about to be realized, Gilmour having promised to go with him to the chief and make the necessary arrangements.

Ulu, too, was pleased. The life at Pisgah was much more irksome to her than that at Pepo-ni. She had found herself restricted in many new ways. Especially she had grown impatient of Mr. Kennedy's persistent dinning in her ears of moral maxims which she could not understand. Even the privilege of being allowed to listen to the music of the harmonium, and the hope of being one day able to join the children in singing hymns, could not quite atone for the wearisome discipline to which she was sometimes subjected. Then, much as she adored Kate, the bibi could never be to her as the Bwana mzungu, to whom she was now more than ever devoted since he had saved her from the lion's dreadful jaws.

As the little party moved westward in the

direction of Kindi, each one silently followed his or her own thoughts, or, when the nature of the pathway permitted it, indulged in desultory snatches of conversation. As they approached Pepo-ni, the father and daughter fell to discussing the character of Gilmour, and the chances of establishing a mission at Seri's, just as they had done nearly two months before at the same spot. Even yet Mr. Kennedy and Kate could not quite agree on the former topic. Though inclined to form a much higher estimate of him than at first, Gilmour was still largely incomprehensible to the missionary, and, not being able to view him except through the medium of his own practical nature, he sometimes said hard things about him. On these occasions, as already said, his daughter warmly espoused the cause of her new-found friend. She admitted that his present do-nothing life was indefensible; but then, she argued, it was only the symptom of a temporary disease, not the outcome of a permanent state of mind.

"It's only an unusually deep fit of 'the blues,' papa," she said. "He is fast recovering. You'll see he will soon go home."

"It's all very well to talk about 'fits of the blues,'" grumbled Mr. Kennedy. "For my part, I don't profess to understand them. Nobody not utterly devoid of common sense would allow them-

selves to give way to your so-called 'fits.' Humph!
A nice plague such an atrabiliar temperament
must be!"

"To the owner of it in particular," said Kate,
laughing at her father's dissatisfied tone. "It
can't bring him much happiness. Or perhaps I
should rather say," she added, correcting herself,
"it will bring him an ever-recurring round of
pain, discontent, and disappointment. Only when
his happiness does come, he will feel it, like his
sorrows, more keenly than other people."

"Humph!" grumbled Mr. Kennedy again.

"You will see it's just as I say," Kate resumed.
"Mr. Gilmour is extremely sensitive and very
romantic. He has had lots of grand dreams and
high aspirations, and somehow or another they've
been disappointed. Perhaps he expected too much
or attempted to soar too high. At any rate, he
has had a terrible fall."

"What else could you expect? A nature such
as you describe will always fail, because finding its
sole inspiration in itself and in the world."

Kate made no reply, beyond a scarcely per-
ceptible shrug of the shoulders, which eloquently
said that, however good might be the understanding
between her father and herself, there were yet
some things which they could not view from the
same standpoint.

The pathway now became narrow and difficult, and Mr. Kennedy gradually fell some distance behind. Kate grew flushed and tired, and silently sighed a wish that she was once more in the cool shades of Pepo-ni.

" Ulu," she called, " where are you ? "

" Iko (here), bibi," replied the girl, tripping lightly to the donkey's side.

" How far are we from Pepo-ni ? "

" We shall reach it when the sun—— "

" Well ? When the sun is—where ? " queried Kate, looking round to see where Ulu would point to. " Why, what is it ? " she cried, suddenly drawing rein, as she beheld Ulu standing rigid and speechless, a look of horror on her face.

Her answer was a blood-curdling yell, as from behind tree and bush sprang forth a horrid array of naked savages. It was now Kate's turn to stand mute and terror-stricken, a scream which shaped itself in her throat dying away in a faint murmur.

But if Kate and Ulu were dumb, not so the donkey-boy. His hereditary instinct was a stronger force than any fear, and the Chaga cry which signals danger and calls to arms rang out through the woods with thrilling effect, till transformed into a death-groan as half a dozen huge spears buried themselves in the boy's writhing body. He fell at the feet of Tanga, who sniffed him wonderingly; while Kate, scarcely knowing what she did, fumbled involuntarily in her revolver pocket for the weapon she was seldom without.

At that moment her father's voice rang out behind her in tones of wild alarm. "Kate! Kate!" he cried in agony.

Startled into new life, Kate turned with an answering cry, only to see an upraised spear, and hear the shout of triumph that went ringing through the forest as the fell weapon did its bloody office. Forgetful of her impotency, and heedless of her danger, Kate jumped frantically from Tanga's back to fly to her father's aid. A gleaming circle of spears hemmed her in. To pass was impossible. Wildly she looked around her. Useless! There was no loophole anywhere. The tension on her feelings grew too strong; her body was too weak for the spirit it contained. She reeled a moment, steadied herself, and looked round once more, then staggered and fell fainting on the ground.

Meanwhile Ulu had narrowly escaped sharing the fate of Mr. Kennedy and the donkey-boy, a warrior having made a playful lunge at her with his spear. Happily she was too quick for him, and sprang aside in time to avoid the thrust. Again, in more deadly earnest, he raised his bloody weapon. Hurriedly Ulu gasped out something in the Masai language. The warrior changed his mind, and instead of killing made her prisoner.

For the moment Kate's safety was assured by the astonishment evoked by her strange appearance. Round her prostrate body the warriors crowded excitedly, expressing their surprise in wondering stares and exclamations. Was she some strange animal? Was she Ngai (God)? Timidly they touched her clothes, every instant fearing some dread manifestation.

Time was precious, however. The Masai had none to waste on idle speculations. The war-cry raised by the donkey-boy was being rapidly taken up on all sides, and, their presence thus prematurely discovered, they must beat a hasty retreat.

" Kill it ! " commanded the lytunu (leader).

" Ēō," promptly replied his men.

" Hai! hai! " (hold) screamed Ulu, as spears and bloodstained clubs were ruthlessly raised over Kate's prostrate form. " That is Ngai. That is the god of Kibo ! " she added explanatorily.

With exclamations of amazement and awe, the Masai shrank back in fear, their arms hanging paralyzed by their sides.

Ulu was thoroughly equal to the occasion. Struggling from the hands of her captors, she sprang lightly to Kate's side, and confronted the warriors with the air of a savage queen.

"I am Ulu," she cried, "daughter of Ngaré (the streamlet) and the lybon Simba. I now belong to the spirit of Kibo."

Renewed exclamations greeted this announcement, and the savages looked on Ulu with additional respect.

"Go!" continued the little heroine, with supreme audacity. "Go, and leave Ngai to return to his abode in peace, lest he cut off the rains from your pastures and your cattle die."

Uncertain what to do, the Masai looked towards their leader for orders.

"No," he cried; "if indeed this is Ngai, he shall go with us. He will make us bold in battle, and our spears shall continually drip with blood. He will live with us, and our fields shall prosper, and the udders of our cows shall burst with milk."

This audacious resolution was hailed with acclamations. It fired the savage imagination to think of taking home a god.

With quick perception, Ulu saw at a glance it was useless to attempt to brave their captors, and she turned to Kate, who now began to show signs of returning consciousness. The warriors fell back, fearing the possible consequences of their temerity. They laid aside their arms, and would have thrown themselves prostrate before her, but that, never having known a superior being to whom to render homage, they had not learned the significance of bowed knee or faces humbled in the dust. In their own rude fashion, however, they showed the feelings which possessed them. Plucking up handfuls of grass—their most sacred object—they held it towards the supposed god, thus swearing in their own way that their intentions were friendly. At the same time they made a slight sputtering noise with their lips, as if they would spit upon her, meaning thereby to deprecate her wrath and solicit her goodwill.

Kate had swooned away surrounded by cruel-faced savages and murderous spears—she awoke to consciousness to find the same savages weaponless, and holding tufts of grass in their black, oily palms, while they went through the form of spitting upon her. The oft-repeated word "Ngai! Ngai!" fell upon her ear with no special significance for the moment. She seemed to be in some terrible nightmare that was never coming to an end.

"Pick up some grass, bibi," prompted Ulu earnestly in Ki-Swahili.

Mechanically Kate obeyed, and immediately a joyous shout burst from the expectant warriors. Ngai had declared himself the friend of the Masai! A new era of successful warfare, of blood flowing in torrents, not to speak of abundance of meat and milk, was about to commence.

It was now time to move onwards. Though five minutes had not yet elapsed since the war-cry had first been raised, Chaga was already alarmed, and at any moment a fight might ensue. Tanga was at once laid hold of, and passively Kate allowed herself to be placed in the saddle. More dead than alive, she was rapidly conveyed down the hill. Once at the bottom and on safer ground, the Masai gave vent to their feelings in a shout of joy and victory, and pranced around the donkey in jubilant delight. Group after group joined the exultant throng to take up the cry of " Ngai!" and unite in the ecstatic dance. As the main body of the Masai army was reached the shout went up which had been heard by Gilmour.

With such a precious capture the warriors did not dare to linger, thinking the Wa-Chaga would certainly attempt the rescue of their god. The camp, therefore, was struck at once, and the march towards Masai-land resumed.

When at length Kate fully realized that she was being carried away a prisoner, she was taken possession of by a horrible fear of the possible fate in store for her. For a moment every other feeling was lost in horror. Then a strange, hard light came into her eyes, and a look of proud determination settled on her face. " Better death than *that!* " she said to herself, as she felt that her revolver was safe and loaded in her pocket.

Kate's situation was sufficiently hopeless. What had she to expect from these licentious, bloodthirsty savages, the indulgence of whose brutal passions was their sole rule in life? Better a thousand times have shared the fate of her father than thus be reserved for worse. With the thought of the old man murdered came a pang of keenest sorrow, and the girl's surcharged feelings at last found relief in tears.

She could not conjure up the slightest ray of hope. There was no chance of escape, no third course between death and dishonour. Even as Kate came to this conclusion, the report of a rifle rang sharp and clear from the side of the mountain. A sudden wild thought of rescue flashed across her mind, and eagerly she scanned the forest. Nothing was to be seen. Another report followed. This time Kate saw the rising smoke. The warriors, in momentary confusion, crowded round her. A white handkerchief was waved in the air.

" It is Mr. Gilmour," she cried involuntarily.

A derisive shout rose from the Masai. Plucking out her own handkerchief, Kate gave it a single wave. The next moment it was torn from her grasp. What mattered that, however? Mr. Gilmour knew her position; he would not desert her. There was comfort in the thought; she would not despair yet.

CHAPTER VI.

THE Masai warriors among whom Kate Kennedy had so disastrously fallen formed the main body of a raiding army which had been to the coast. There they had made great captures of cattle, and as an incidental amusement killed a considerable number of men, women, and children. Flushed with success, they were on their way homeward; and now, to give further *éclat* to their triumph, they had, as they imagined, captured a spirit or god.

We cannot attempt to follow Kate through all the terrors, sorrows, and hardships it was now her lot to experience. Her worst fears were dispelled when Ulu explained in what light they regarded her, while the killing march under the fierce sun somewhat deadened her anguish of mind on thinking of the terrible fate of her father.

In their own rough way the Masai showed themselves full of consideration. They carefully led the donkey by easy paths, and lent assistance at the numerous streams and rivers which, with some difficulty and danger, had to be crossed. More dead than alive, Miss Kennedy reached the river Kikavo, and there happily the Masai camped for the night.

In the feasting which followed, the warriors did not forget the necessities of their captive. They brought her blood drawn from the veins of newly killed cattle, and remarked with amazement her shuddering repulsion of this their choicest drink. Equally incomprehensible was her rejection of their finest chunks of beef, which, half raw, half charred, they proffered, spitted on spear-points, or, worse still, in their filthy hands.

Happily Ulu came to the rescue, and sent the well-intentioned but obnoxious savages to the right-about. The little maiden now proved a veritable god-send to Kate. Though so young in years as compared with the latter, she was yet much older in all the rude experience of life. She took the bibi in a manner under her protection, and was at once her friend, her guardian, and her hand-maiden. In her proud position as " slave of Ngai " and interpreter of his wishes, she was obeyed by the elmoran (warriors) as they had never obeyed woman before, and she took advantage of the respect with which they regarded her to render Kate's position as comfortable as possible, and

secure her from obnoxious attentions and repulsive
intrusions on her privacy.

Ulu herself, it must be confessed, rather enjoyed
the position in which she now found herself.

She felt at home and in congenial surroundings
among the Masai warriors, and, absolved by circumstances from the irksome customs of Pepo-ni,
she gave free rein to her wild nature and instincts.
Indeed, during the continued captivity of the next
few weeks, the only check to a complete return
in every particular to the savage life was the
presence of Kate.

The second day's march lay through open wooded
country and proved somewhat more pleasant than
that of the day before. Towards evening a halt
was made near Kibo-noto, midway between Kilimanjaro and Mount Meru, those two great mountain
masses fancifully regarded by the Wa-Swahili as
the pillars which form the gateway to Masai-land.

Here a couple of days were spent, so as to allow
a number of small flying parties to join the main
army and add to the pomp and circumstance of
the return home.

The district of Sigirari in which the Masai were
now camped lies at a height of nearly six thousand
feet, and is in consequence comparatively cold at
night. Here Kate would have suffered greatly had
it not been for Ulu, who at once, with trained

dexterity, set about constructing a dome-shaped hut of bent branches, over which she threw the hides of oxen. A couch of grass having been placed in the extemporized dwelling, Kate entered into possession, greatly to the increase of her comfort in more ways than one. It not only proved useful as a means of shelter, but also served as a refuge from the crowding warriors who hourly pressed round their much-enduring prisoner, and sometimes would have invaded even the privacy of the hut had not Ulu mounted guard over the small hole which did duty as a door, and kept them at a respectful distance, declaring that Ngai was making madawa (medicines), and must not be disturbed on pain of terrible consequences. Even this excuse would not always serve, however, and Kate, making a virtue of necessity, was fain to appear at the door holding a tuft of grass in her hand, in pledge of amity.

By noon of the second day all the elmoran had assembled at the appointed rendezvous. There was, therefore, no reason for further delay, and it was determined that the army should make its entry on the following morning. As an appropriate finish to the campaign a grand feast was appointed for the afternoon.

To that end a number of the fattest cattle were selected from the herd, and, with boisterous cries

and much pricking of spears, driven into camp.
With savage glee the warriors goaded the already
half-wild cattle to madness. Frantically the poor
brutes tried to escape or knock down their tor-
mentors, only to find their legs entangled in hide
ropes, and amid a general heightening of the
hilarious excitement sink exhausted beneath a rain
of cruel stabs and stunning blows from heavily
swung clubs.

The oxen, once bound and helpless, the butchers
emulated each other in trying the hardness of their
fists and their strength of muscle, in attempts
to fell the poor brutes at a blow. Where fists
were unsuccessful, clubs soon settled the bloody
business.

No sooner was a felled ox down than, like a
pack of half-starved hyænas, the warriors threw
themselves upon it with fiendish cries, and cut the
veins open with their knives. As the blood gushed
out warm and red, they fastened themselves to
the cuts and sucked with horrible relish, making
inarticulate sounds expressive of their inhuman
satisfaction, while their bloodshot eyes glared ferociously, and they clung with their hands to the
yielding skin of their victim.

Their enjoyment seemed to be heightened by
feeling the animal's still warm flesh quivering in
their mouths, and its last convulsive throes under

their naked, clinging bodies as its life-blood ebbed away.

In the unbridled desire to drink many lost patience and temper, and struggled with threatening voice and gesture to dislodge those who had secured a place before them. The men thus disturbed turned upon the others like fiends incarnate, and clubs were drawn and spears lifted with apparently murderous intent.

Some of the warriors, however, proceeded in a more methodical and dignified manner. The ox being stunned, they skinned a large part of the neck in such a way that the hide, when properly held, formed a basin or receptacle for the blood. The jugular vein was then severed and its reeking contents allowed to gush into the extemporized basin, to which the feasters applied themselves with loathsome avidity.

The edge of their horrible appetite thus taken off, they became possessed with a species of madness or intoxication, dashing blood on each other with fiendish hilarity, or bathing their faces in the reeking fluid.

Ulu, from her post at Kate's house, watched the scene with strange fascination. As the terrible orgy developed, her dilated eyes glistened, her heart throbbed with tenfold force, all the latent savagery of her nature struggling up within her,

and urging her to join the feast. · For the moment
she forgot utterly her life of the past two months.
Gilmour, Pepo-ni, and the Bibi were alike non-
existent. Her whole being was concentrated in the
scene before her, and she would have run to throw
herself among the brutal throng, but the very
strength of her feelings held her for a time chained
to the spot. At length, slowly and mechanically,
as if actuated by some will other than her own,
she rose from her sitting posture, and step by step,
began moving forward, drawn irresistibly towards
the bloody revel.

"Ulu!"

With a gasp and shiver, Ulu stopped paralyzed,
suddenly recalled to a sense of her position by the
sound of the Bibi's voice. She stood a moment
irresolute.

"Ulu! Ulu! Where are you?" cried Kate
again in a somewhat dismayed tone, at the same
time hastening to the door and looking out. Ulu
turned shamefacedly, and, not daring to look up,
came back to the hut. Kate had seen enough of
what was going on in the camp to enable her to
guess correctly the nature of the temptation by
which her little handmaiden had been assailed.
Gently she drew the poor child away from the
sight of the ghastly carnival and into the quiet
and darkness of the tent, where for long she sat

talking to her of Gilmour, telling her, since she could not make clear to the girl's unenlightened intellect what there would have been wrong in itself in joining such a feast, how much it would have vexed both the Bwana and Kate herself, had she done so.

All the while Kate was in a painful condition of dread lest the warriors in their madness should intrude upon her and insist on her joining them. She had got one or two glimpses of the earlier phases of the feast, and had sickened with horror at the disgusting scenes. Happily, however, she was too much feared, or else for the moment was forgotten, and, to her intense relief, she was left unmolested.

Meanwhile the brutal appetites of the feasters took a new turn. The last drop of blood drained from the cattle, they set upon the carcases with renewed energies, hacking them with their swords, tearing them limb from limb, and tugging and quarrelling over the pieces like dogs, each one anxious to secure the choicest parts, among which was specially reckoned the fat.

Soon the camp had the aspect of shambles. Bullock's heads, cut open to abstract the brains and tongues, lay everywhere, mingling in ghastly confusion with half-denuded ribs and disgusting offal. Everybody and everything were bespattered with blood and shreds of flesh. An overpowering smell of roasting and burning beef permeated the air.

Over the fires the yet hungry Masai sat impatiently watching the cooking meat, or, unable to restrain their appetites, gloated over half-raw chunks, which they tore with their fang-like teeth. A few, more epicurean in their tastes, broke marrow-bones, and sucked their contents with supreme relish.

As their hunger gradually became appeased, the warriors grew more expansive and genial, and testified to their complaisant mood by playfully snatching away the pieces of beef their neighbours were bent on carrying to their mouths, or indulged in the edifying pastime of bickering one another with lumps of flesh. Picking up leg-bones or ribs, they sparred with each other, or, using them as drumsticks, whacked them on the burning logs of wood in time to a howled-out war-song.

Gradually the gorging began to tell, and, stretching themselves out on the ground, the revellers one by one fell asleep, breathing with difficulty from over-feeding, and snoring in sonorous concert, while lumps of forgotten beef burned to cinders in the fires.

As evening began to draw its shadows over the disgusting scene, the herd of captured cattle were driven back to camp by the herdsmen—mostly weaklings and boys, who were thus compelled to serve the stronger.

Snarling viciously at being disturbed, the warriors bestirred themselves to make room for the cattle in the centre of the camp. The poor brutes, with finer feelings than their masters, required to be driven with imprecations and blows among the remains of their lately slaughtered kind. To prevent them straying, and as a safeguard against the numerous wild beasts, the Masai now disposed themselves in a circle round the animals, and once more settled themselves to sleep.

As darkness set in the feasting was resumed, in a minor way. More than ever did the scene resemble something not of this world. The lurid glow of the fires, with their tongues of flame and curling columns of smoke; the half-seen forms of the warriors, looking preternaturally savage in the uncertain light; within the camp, the restless, terror-stricken cattle, snorting and lowing; without, the circle of intense darkness, lightened only by the gleaming eyes of hyænas, and vocal with a continuous concert of howls, hardly distinguishable from the utterances of the human hyænas inside; —all these made up a scene impossible adequately to picture or describe.

There are limits to all human powers, even to

the eating capacities of Masai warriors. As the night advanced, the feasters, gorged and surfeited, arranged themselves for sleep.. Most of them simply rolled over on their backs, regardless of comfort; but others, more luxurious in their tastes, rolled up raw hides as pillows, or drew them, wet and bloody, over their naked bodies.

Long before midnight the entire camp was asleep, with the exception of the men who had borne the heat and labour of the day, and who now had to watch over the slumbers of their companions.

The medley of wild-beast cries became more insistent than ever. Their appetites, whetted to a painful degree by the scent of blood and flesh, rendered the animals furious, and urged them to make bold dashes towards cast-aside bones or offal, only to be driven back by the flaring firebrands hurled at them by the guards.

Worn out with the horrors of the day, Kate fell at length into a troubled sleep. Suddenly she woke with a painful start and sensation of fright, to find herself in utter darkness and unable to see anything. Had she only been dreaming? she asked herself, possessed nevertheless by a vague feeling that some danger threatened. She held her breath and listened, but she could hear nothing. With straining eyes she sought to pierce the pitch darkness of the hut. In vain; there was nothing to be seen.

Kate was about to lie down again when suddenly something which had blocked the doorway moved noiselessly aside. As the lights from the fires streamed in, Kate saw with a shudder the vaguely outlined form of what appeared to be a Masai warrior in the hut. With a scream she sank back, and hardly knowing what she did, fired off her revolver. But even as she screamed the word "Gilmour" reached her bewildered ear, and struck her dumb.

"Oh, bibi! bibi! Silence! It is I, Uledi," came from the darkness.

Immediately Kate's fears were turned into horrified anticipation of the consequences of the precipitate alarm. There was no time to think what was to be done.

Already the sentinels were at the door, desirous of knowing the meaning of the unusual sounds, and Kate and Uledi lay hardly daring to breathe, crouched in the darkest corner of the hut. Ulu, however, with her usual promptitude, was equal to the occasion.

"Go," she cried, "and leave Ngai in peace. He dreams and speaks with the spirits of Kibo."

The savages were quite well pleased to accept this explanation, and, awestruck, resumed their posts.

A rapid exchange of questions and answers now took place. Her father only wounded and getting

better, and Gilmour following the Masai, waiting
his opportunity to effect her rescue ; nay, at that
moment not a hundred yards off;—that was, indeed,
news to reanimate Kate's heart and suffuse her
eyes with grateful tears. In addition to his re-
assuring messages Gilmour, with the utmost forethought, had sent Kate a small kid-skin bag,
containing a few necessaries, such as salt, an
article not used by the Masai.

Having gleaned from the bibi and Ulu all they
could tell about their destination in Masai-land,
and satisfied himself as to how they were being
treated, Uledi prepared to leave. With grateful
warmth Kate grasped the hand of the faithful
Zanzibari, but could find no appropriate words
in which to express her gratitude either to him or
to his master. "Tell the Bwana," she began, but
ere her quivering lips could complete this sentence,
Uledi had kissed her hand after the fashion of
Swahili slaves, and with a whispered "Please God,
we will rescue you," was gone. A moment's survey
sufficed to assure him that the coast was clear, and
he glided out and into a deep shadow unseen.

To the profound astonishment of Kate, who
watched him anxiously, Uledi did not make straight
for the woods. Under cover of the shadow and
then of a small bush, he approached one of the
fires where there happened to be no watchers.

Here he disposed himself as if to sleep. Some one near him yawned and moved. Uledi, with a lazy gesture, drew his kid-skin covering over his face. Soon the savage snored. No one else was moving. One, two, three minutes passed—hours apparently to Kate. Then Uledi sat up. He also yawned, and gave himself the air of being restless and unable to sleep. Kate could hardly repress an exclamation as she saw him at length stand up and stretch himself. Instinctively she looked around. No one seemed to notice him. Then carelessly, without any concealment, Uledi walked coolly out of the camp, Kate watching him with palpitating heart and fascinated gaze.

A minute later, the tension of her feelings relaxed, as, amid the howling of the hyænas, she heard from the forest three hoots of an owl, which told that master and man had met; and Kate, feeling a new hope of life, turned in to sleep soundly till daybreak.

CHAPTER VII.

WHEN morning broke after the eventful night we have described, the Masai warriors were in no hurry to bestir themselves. They awoke looking weary and stupid, as even Masai will if they go to sleep with overloaded stomachs. The chilly air, however, had the effect of making them gather round the fires, where, looking anything but warlike, they shivered and crouched like any miserable Wā-nyika.

Meanwhile, their captive was also awake, making, for the first time since her capture, an attempt at a toilette, and hungrily drinking some milk which before dawn Ulu had been able to draw from an old and somewhat subdued cow.

As the rising sun began to dispel the raw fogs of morning and warm the atmosphere, the warriors gradually acquired more life and began to prepare for the march. To appear in good form before the women and attract their favourable attention, they rubbed themselves well over with hot pieces

of fat till their skins glistened again, after which
they painted themselves with various colours, till
they looked caricatures of humanity.   To add to the
effect, they made various figures on their legs and
bodies, by drawing a finger through the paint.   A
few dandies, better provided with the luxuries of
Masai cosmetics, plastered themselves thickly with
a stiff mixture of grease and clay, till, looking the
most repulsive of bloated beings, they stood, the
admiration and envy of the entire army.   Thus
clothed, they next rolled up their small kid-skin
karosses—which usually ornamented rather than
covered their shoulders in times of peace—and tied
them round their waist like a belt.   Monkey-skins
or capes formed of feathers were donned instead,
and their faces were framed in an elliptically-
shaped adornment of nodding ostrich plumes.
Down their backs hung the war-cloth, or nāiberi,
the dress being completed by the addition of
encircling straps of colobus-skin round the ankles
and calves of their legs.   At the ankles the straps
bore small projecting wings forcibly reminding one
of Mercury's appendages.   The simé, or sword, and
rungu, or club, were next attached to the waist-
band, and then, with his huge, device-ornamented
shield in one hand, and murderous spear in the
other, each Masai was ready for the road.

In the mean time, Ulu had captured Tanga, and,

amidst a circle of admiring savages, had contrived, with the help of Kate, to put on the saddle. Her mistress mounted, Ulu took her station by the donkey's side, the warriors fell into marching order, and the procession set forward toward the interior of Masai land.

For a couple of hours the way lay through a pleasant interchange of wood and glade, till the forest was entirely left behind, and the army entered a great rolling grassy plain, which extended away to the far distance, where it was bounded by a range of mountains that stretched, amphitheatre-wise, from the pillars of the mlango, Kilimanjaro and Meru.

At first this rich and fertile region appeared to be given over wholly to big game. Rhinoceroses, buffaloes, zebra, wildebeest, antelopes, ostriches, were everywhere to be seen in astonishing numbers, in herds, groups, or solitary, according to the habits of the particular animal.

After a time evidences of other inhabitants could be descried, in the shape of dark, circular objects, from which rose curling smoke. These, Kate speedily learned, were Masai kraals. At once the warriors began to fall into more military order. An advance guard was formed, having the captured cattle in the centre, and headed by four small flying parties; behind came the rear-guard, with Kate and Ulu in its midst.

As they approached the kraals of Kiraragwa, a great commotion was observable among the inhabitants. Old men and women gathered in groups outside the gate, and men and boys ran from place to place, eager to spread the news of the warriors' return.

At a given signal the entire army struck up a song of victory, which burst upon that silent plain with a magnificently wild effect, and rolled to the base of Kilimanjaro, to be returned in mocking echoes. The chief lytunu, or army leader, led off with a chanted recitative, which recounted with much imaginative genius the great deeds of himself and his followers. Each stanza was followed by a chorus from the entire army, thanking Ngāi and Mbaratian (their chief medicine man) for enabling them to kill so many miserable people.

Meanwhile men, women, and children were hurrying out in great excitement to welcome their returning kinsfolk.

No sooner had the home-staying el-moran (warriors) arrived within a few hundred yards of their more adventurous brethren, than parties of the latter detached themselves and rushed at the former in well-simulated fury. Shaking their spears in the air, and nodding their feather headdresses defiantly, they pranced and sprang about with derisive cries, daring the pretended enemy to come and fight. The challenge was taken up with immense spirit, and as the opposing parties closed the surrounding plain assumed all the appearance of a battle-field, so great was the exciting clamour, so numerous and deadly seemed the hand-to-hand encounters.

In the midst of the mimic fights the women painfully hobbled up, heavily handicapped by their extraordinary leggings of thick iron wire, which reached from the ankle to the knee, and by their stiffness and excessive weight (frequently ten pounds each) prevented their wearers from moving with any degree of freedom. Joining the men, they added their shrill and strident screams to the chorus of welcome, and forming groups, advanced with curious jerky movements, clapping their hands in time to their song.

In the first general commotion Kate remained unnoticed ; but speedily the news spread that Ngāi, the god from Kibo, had been captured. The cries of incredulity which had at first greeted this intelligence, speedily gave place to exclamations of wonder and awe when attention was directed to the rear, where, true enough, a something white and marvellous could be seen amidst the surrounding crowd. The excited clamour died into silence, only broken by feeble, awe-struck ejaculations of "Hāi! hāi!" and sons or sweethearts were deserted, as picking up tufts of grass, the women painfully hobbled off to see this new phenomenon.

Not yet knowing how near it might be safe to approach a god, they kept at a respectful distance. Mute and motionless they stood gazing with dilated eyes at this strange being of extraordinary shape (Kate's dress, as usual, being at first taken for part of herself), and riding an animal which resembled a donkey, yet was so different from any they had ever seen. Ngai, however, did not look terrible or wicked, and gradually the spectators acquired more confidence.

At length some one among the women, more courageous than the rest, struck up a chanted prayer in a shrill and plaintive voice. One by one the others joined in, till from front to rear of that savage array one mighty cry arose, which caused even distant antelopes to cease their grazing or their gambols, and turning, seek with head uplifted and ears cocked, the cause of the unwonted volume of sound which rolled over the usually silent plain.

After this unpremeditated demonstration, the surging crowd, somewhat calmed down, once more moved forward.

Somewhat after midday they reached the sparkling Ngaré N'Erobi (cold stream), where they halted some time to refresh themselves, while the fighting party gave an account of their successful raid to

the el-morūū (elders or married men). This must
needs be done in decency and order, and not with
the noise and gabble of women and lajomba (Wa-
Swahili).

The elders, comparatively decently clothed in
handsome karosses of grey monkey-skins or of skins
of the tree hyrax sewn together, ranged themselves
on one side, their bows and arrows—the weapons
of married men—lying at their feet. The warriors
placed themselves opposite, their spears sticking
in the ground and shields rested against them.
The women ceased their talk, or retired some
distance, and for a space there was silence.

Then a warrior rose. All eyes were turned
expectantly upon him, for the lygonani, or orator
of the army, was about to speak. Leisurely he
plucked his spear from the ground and his blood-
stained club from his belt. Then, striking an easy
attitude, he gave a final look around, as if he
would solicit the attention and the indulgence of
his hearers. In a low, quiet voice, so pleasant to
hear, so unlike the man who spoke, he commenced
to narrate the gathering of the clans, and the
march to the coast, their hunting ground. As he
proceeded, his delivery became more animated and
his voice more impassioned, while he described
the various daring feats they had performed in
capturing cattle and slaughtering Wa-nyika and

Wa-Swahili. The eyes of his hearers glistened with the pride of battle as the various incidents of the raid were vividly brought back to their memories. Uninterrupted, however, the lygonani was allowed to display his oratorical powers, and to give due effect to his glowing periods with effectively wielded club, till he reached his climax in detailing the capture of Kate, and amid a variety of applausive grunts sat down.

Another pause ensued. An elder of importance then took up the word. Speaking with even more dignity and composure than the lygonani, he welcomed the warriors home, and congratulated them on their achievements. Coming, however, to their striking feat of capturing Ngai, he doubted the prudence of the step. The gods were not to be touched with impunity. It might bring fortune or it might bring dire calamity. That had still to be seen. His advice was that Ngai should be treated with the utmost respect, lest he turn against his captors, and sweep off their cattle by disease, or render them sterile and the warriors' arms weak.

Looks of profound dismay stole over the faces of the el-moran, as the possible consequences of the feat, which they now saw was foolhardy, were gloomily depicted.

In the midst of the consternation which ensued, a second elder rose and addressed the assemblage

in words of similar import. He revived the drooping spirits of the warriors, however, by pointing
out, as a matter of hopeful augury, that Ngai must
have been willing to come thus among them, or
he would easily have scattered the warriors before
him as dust before the wind. What more probable
than that, sick of living among such slaves as the
Wa-Chaga, he had wished to come among heroes
and bloodshedders like themselves? He also drew
encouragement from the fact that in their kins-
woman, Ulu, daughter of Simba, they had one who
could speak to Ngai, and ascertain his wishes and
what he approved or disapproved. He—the elder—
therefore earnestly urged the importance of con-
sulting Ulu in all matters, lest in anything they
should offend the captured deity.

The warriors looked somewhat relieved, and
broke into muttered approbation as the elder sat
down.

Meanwhile, Kate was resting near at hand under
the cool shade of a sycamore tree. She was overcome by fatigue, and would have slept, but for the
crowd of women and children who gathered around
her. Some brought milk, and gave it to Ulu for
Ngai; but as the calabashes in which it was contained had never been touched with water for years,
and had only been kept *clean* by a daily rinsing
with wood ashes to prevent the new supplies of milk

from being infected and soured, Kate's senses revolted against the refreshment so served up.

Children were pushed towards her to be "blessed" in the peculiar manner to which we have already made allusion, and on Ulu's urgent appeals, Kate reluctantly brought herself to go through the form required, to the rapturous delight of the highly favoured and happy mothers.

After a couple of hours the march was resumed. Kate remarked with relief that the warriors were more respectful, and Ulu was made still more proud and impudent by having a donkey assigned to her, to enable her to ride alongside her master, Ngai.

But for the dryness of the atmosphere, and the elevation of the country over which they were now passing, Kate could never have survived the burning sun and the fatigues of the march. Happily also the breeze from the mountains swept cool and refreshing over the plain, scarcely less welcome to the traveller, that it raised disagreeable clouds of dust.

Towards evening the army took possession of a vacated kraal, which, having also been a huge fold for cattle, had very much the appearance of a gigantic dunghill. Luckily the weather had been dry and scorching, and Kate was too much exhausted to be fastidious or more than vaguely observant of her surroundings, as she was conducted to the best hut in the place.

Next day an equally fatiguing march lay before them. But Kate began to be inured to the hardships of travel, and, with mind more at ease, she helped to pass the time and keep her mind occupied by noting the strange scenes which passed before her. Now and then she conversed cheerfully with Ulu, and as it was to Gilmour they looked for rescue, very naturally he was the most frequent subject of conversation.

In one of these talks Ulu did not hesitate to ask Kate in a very embarrassing manner why he treated her (Ulu) as he did, being, as she was, his wife. Kate, rather put out, tried to explain Gilmour's intentions and projects, but failed even more signally than that young man himself in making Ulu understand what it was to be "like the wives of the white men."

"He wants to make you like me," Kate explained, with a smile.

Ulu's only answer was to look up with wide-open eyes and incredulity expressed in every lineament. Become like the bibi! Was such a miracle possible even to the wonder-working white men? What madawa (medicine) would be given, or potent uchawi (black magic) employed to transform her into the semblance of her mistress? No; Ulu rejected the notion as impossible. But the conversation had suggested a new idea.

" Won't the Bwana marry you some day ? " she asked.

" Marry me ! " exclaimed Kate. " Good gracious, mtoto, what put that into your head ? "

" He is very rich. Oh, so rich ! He will be able to give your father plenty of goods in exchange for you."

" But then, you see, I don't want to marry."

" Don't want to marry ! " cried Ulu, astounded at such an unheard-of notion. " Why, what could you do without a husband ? "

" Oh, I shall do very well," was Kate's unsatisfactory answer, puzzled how otherwise to reply to the simple little maid.

" But won't your father give you away, whether you want or not ? "

" Oh dear, no ! Fathers among the wazungu never do that sort of thing."

Ulu remained silent, mentally contrasting the ways of wazungu with those of Wa-Chaga, the latter of whom only look upon their daughters as marketable commodities, to be disposed of at the suitable time to the highest bidder.

" But if your father should die," she at length resumed, " won't some white man seize you and make you his wife or his slave, or sell you to another ? "

Kate smiled good-naturedly, amused in spite of

herself and in spite of her surroundings, by the girl's ingenuous ignorance. "No fear of that, mtoto," she said. "White people never make slaves, and therefore no white man would touch me. Besides, the men in Ulyiah like to make themselves the servants of the women."

Again Ulu was silent, partly with astonishment, partly because she was pondering what could be the bibi's motive in telling such extraordinary lies. That Ulu should suspect Kate of falsehood is not to be wondered at, for the Frenchman's saying, that "speech was given us to conceal our thoughts," is something more than a phrase among all negro tribes, among whom nothing is more admired than the gift of skilful lying on all occasions. After an unavailing attempt to imagine a state of society in which women were the superiors or even the equals of men, she resumed the conversation.

"Well, I should like the Bwana to marry you."

"Indeed!" said Kate, amused at the girl's notion, and anxious to hear more of marriage from Ulu's point of view.

"You would be his chief wife, you know, because an mzungu, like himself. I would be the next, because the daughter of the chief of Kindi, and first married. We would make the other wives he would marry do all our work and be our servants. That would be splendid, wouldn't it?"

The idea of becoming one among a host of Wa-Chaga wives was irresistible, and, for the moment forgetting her situation, Kate laughed outright. Despairing, however, of making Ulu understand the impossibility of the proposed scheme, she remained silent, and soon became absorbed in the train of ideas aroused by the crude notions of her simple companion.

Ulu, receiving no reply, and misunderstanding the expression of amusement which still hovered about Kate's lips, thought the bibi was nibbling at the bait, and set herself to think out in more detail the management of Gilmour's future harem. That he would eventually marry a great number of girls she could not permit herself to doubt. He, a man so young and so rich, be content with only one or even two wives! Pooh! It was inconceivable. She would have little pride in being head of such a pauper-like establishment. Was not a man held in honour and reputed great in the land according to the number of his wives? And if the Bwana never married any besides herself, would she not be pointed at with scorn and laughter as the sole wife of the mzungu? But how different if she was the next wife to the bibi mzungu, and an array of from fifty to a hundred, or even more, wives beneath her. To have plenty of gorgeous beads and nice cloths was all very well in its way, but to be the second-best wife among a host was infinitely better.

Her imagination warmed at the thought of the delights of power. All unconscious to herself she whacked her donkey vigorously, as if already she had a refractory wife under her stick. At the blow the half-tamed animal rebelliously kicked up its heels in the air and incontinently landed Ulu on the sand, dissipating her dreams for the time being.

On the evening of the third day from Kibo-noto, the Masai reached the Guaso N'Ebor (white stream), at the base of Ndapduk. Here their countrymen were congregated in great numbers, for, being the height of the dry season, the springs on the plains were dried up and the grass scorched. At the base of the mountain it was different, the stream affording an abundant supply of water, around which and on many parts of the precipitous slopes the grass still flourished.

It would be useless to relate the reception the warriors received and the sensation Kate produced, both being similar in kind to what we have already described as marking their arrival at Kiraragwa. Early in the night the captives heard three hoots of an owl, and knowing by that that Gilmour was near them, with a renewed sense of security they slept in peace.

CHAPTER VIII.

IT now behoves us to leave Kate for a time, while we retrace our steps and follow the movements of Gilmour.

On reaching Pepo-ni, after assuring himself of the fate of Miss Kennedy, the first news Gilmour heard, ere he had well passed the gate, was that Mr. Kennedy, whom he had left for dead, was only severely wounded, and had now recovered consciousness. Joyfully Gilmour hastened to the room where the missionary lay, eager to tell him that his daughter still lived. As he entered the house his ardent steps were arrested by the sound of a low moan.

"Oh, God, what have I done? What have I done?" were the anguished words that fell upon his ear, as the missionary turned uneasily on his bed, and feverishly pressed his hands together in an agony of grief and pain.

"Come, come, Mr. Kennedy," said Gilmour, cheerily, as he crossed the threshold. "Don't despair yet. Things are not so bad as they might be."

At the first sound of Gilmour's voice, Kennedy, heedless of the pain of his wound, half rose and turned eagerly towards the door.

"Kate! Where is she?" he gasped out, scarcely able to speak from fear of what the answer might be.

"Safe—at least for the present," returned Gilmour, briefly.

"Thank God for that!" was Mr. Kennedy's pious exclamation as he sank back on the pillows, and for a moment lay with eyes closed as if in prayer. "But where is she?" he asked again, dread once more taking possession of him. "Why does she not come?"

"Hush, Mr. Kennedy; you must be more calm," said Gilmour, soothingly, wondering how he could most gently break the news of Kate's captivity to her almost frantic father.

"Calm?" repeated the sufferer expressively, as he again attempted to raise himself. "I have killed her," he said stonily, after a moment's pause. "Quick, man; out with it!" he cried wildly, paying no heed to Gilmour's repeated attempts to speak. "Tell me the worst at once. She is dead. I knew it;" and, groaning heavily, he sank down again and covered his face with his hands.

"No, no, Mr. Kennedy," said Gilmour, talking as quietly as he could, and laying a restraining hand on his companion's shoulder. "She is *not* dead; she is only a prisoner."

"Only a prisoner!" exclaimed Kennedy, despairingly; "*only* a prisoner! Worse, worse—a thousand times worse!" and, in the anguish of his soul, the missionary cried aloud to God for help in this his time of dire necessity.

"Nonsense, Mr. Kennedy," said Gilmour, assuming an air of cheerfulness, spite of the deep misgiving at his heart. "You really take too black a view of the case. Depend upon it, before long we'll bring her back to you all right. She'll be looked upon as a great lybon (medicine-man); perhaps," he added, as a bright idea struck him, "as Ngai himself. Look what the people here thought about her. You told me yourself they took her for a god. These savages all reason in the same way," he went on consolingly; "everything wonderful is supernatural. You may be quite sure a white woman is too much of a novelty not to be treated with respect, and by the time she has ceased to be a novelty—— Well, we'll have her here by that time," he confidently concluded, his effort to raise the missionary's spirits having helped to lighten his own.

Kennedy shook his head, refusing to be comforted.

He was too weak in body and too much prostrated
in mind, too determined to view everything in its
worst possible light, to pay much heed to Gilmour's
encouraging assurances. In a vague way, however,
he remarked the young man's expressed determination to go to Kate's assistance, and acknowledged it by a pressure of the hand, though
regarding it rather as an expression of goodwill
than a serious promise of effort.

For the time being Gilmour held his peace, while
he proceeded to examine and dress the ugly spear-
wound which had so nearly ended the missionary's
life. Relieved of all apprehensions on Mr. Kennedy's
account, he listened patiently to the narration of
all the circumstances attendant on the birth of
Miss Kennedy and the death of her mother, and to
the torrent of bitter words with which the missionary reproached himself for having, as he said,
sacrificed both wife and daughter to his weak
desire for some sort of companionship in his
exile.

Happily Gilmour diagnosed Kennedy's morbid
mental condition correctly, and in his own mind
formed a more common-sense view of the circumstances of the case. He felt strongly inclined to
tell the worthy man that it was little short of sin
to indulge such exaggerated misgivings, but the
memory of his own recent and similar shortcomings

kept him silent, as unworthy to preach virtue to one in many ways so much better than himself.

The unrestrained outpouring of feeling seemed to do the missionary much good. His tormenting thoughts, once confessed to another, became less intolerable, and he listened eagerly when Gilmour, with intent to console, assured him that he was not to blame for his wife's death or his daughter's present position. As a more pleasant topic of conversation, Gilmour went on to speak hopefully of his plans for effecting Miss Kennedy's rescue, and soon had the satisfaction of seeing his afflicted friend reduced to a calmer and more settled frame of mind. At last, utterly worn out both in brain and body by the fatigue and excitement of the afternoon, the worthy missionary gradually closed his eyes and was soon fast asleep.

Left to his own thoughts, Gilmour did not long remain in a state of inaction. If he was to follow Miss Kennedy and once more restore her to her father, it was clearly time for him to set about making his preparations for the perilous attempt. How was her escape to be effected? Not by force certainly; that was out of the question. Strategy and patient waiting alone could bring about the desired result. He could not formulate any definite plan of campaign, until he knew more exactly Miss Kennedy's position and surroundings in the Masai camp. But these things at least were clear—he must get on the track of the Masai without loss of time, find out where they were bound for, and if possible communicate with Miss Kennedy to let her know that her friends had not forsaken her.

Having made up his mind so far, Gilmour rose with an air of decision, and left the house to consult with Uledi. Calling his faithful headman into the baraza, he unfolded his scheme, such as it was.

"Rapidity and secrecy of movement are the main things, Uledi," he said in conclusion. "I should say we couldn't venture on taking more than four men with us. What do *you* think?"

For a moment Uledi stood silent, staring at his master in open-mouthed surprise. Enter the Masai country with only four men! That was a proposal to take away one's breath.

Gilmour viewed Uledi's astounded expression, and remarked his silence with apprehension.

"Uledi, you are not afraid, are you?" he asked at length.

Uledi looked deeply hurt. "I afraid, Bwana?" he cried indignantly. "When have you known me quail under the eye of the lion? When have you seen me show my back to the Masai? Truly I thought not of the dangers, but only how they might be overcome."

"Then you will go with me?" said Gilmour, briefly.

"Bwana, I go wherever you may lead," was Uledi's solemn protestation. "I know no danger when you are with me."

"Now you are no longer my servant, but my brother," cried Gilmour, touched by the honest fellow's expression of devotion. "Come, though," he continued, suddenly recollecting the urgent necessity for speedy action; "we have no time to waste on words now. Call up the men."

In the shortest possible space of time the men were assembled, and stood waiting to hear the nature of the enterprise to be proposed to them. Uledi stepped forward to address them. With the oratorical skill of a Masai, and the circumlocution and wordiness characteristic of his own race, he very unnecessarily told his audience how the Bibi Kennedy and Ulu had that day been captured by a band of Masai warriors, and that the Bwana was sore at heart for their loss. The Bwana was their father, he went on to say. To him they looked for protection, for food and shelter. From him, too, came their dollars. Could they then sit idly by, he asked, when their master was prostrated with grief? Did not their hearts urge them to do their utmost for his relief?

An unanimous shout here interrupted the perfervid orator. They were one and all the Bwana's wa-toto (children). They would do anything for him. From him they derived their lives; for him they would give them.

"Ngemma!" (good) exclaimed Uledi, with a satisfied air. "The Wa-Swahili are not ungrateful. Now, listen," he went on earnestly. "The Bwana's thoughts are with the bibi and Ulu in Masai-land. He cannot live here while his heart is with them. He must go to them; but he must go secretly, even as the chui (leopard), which, unseen, unheard, steals forth in the night to seek his food. He cannot go alone, however, and he asks four of you —four of his wa-toto—to accompany him, and assist him to bring back his friends."

An eloquent "Oh!" burst from the assembled crowd as Uledi made this astounding announcement. But the wily headman was prepared for the emergency. By a few telling sarcasms directed against one or two well-known cowards, he called forth several bursts of laughter from the crowd, and succeeded in putting the men on their mettle. One after another they volunteered to go, till even the most cowardly came forward with loud protestations of their eagerness to take part in the perilous enterprise. To the well-acted chagrin of the others, three of the bravest and most tried were chosen, Uledi of course constituting the necessary fourth.

This important matter settled, the next consideration was what to take. After much careful deliberation, small loads were arranged thus : One man to carry a small tin kettle and saucepan, with one or two enamelled iron cups, some tea and sugar, four pots of Liebig's Extract, two tins of corn-flour, four pounds of rice, four tins of sardines, a small tin of biscuits, salt, and a few other articles mostly selected with a view to Miss Kennedy's comfort; the members of the rescue party having to depend entirely for their own necessities on what they could capture, shoot, or steal.

The second man carried two rugs, a waterproof sheet of some size, a hammock, and a change of clothes for the captives—a luxury Gilmour would not have been able to provide had it not been that, after the attack that afternoon, one of his men had luckily discovered among the bushes a small bag containing a dress and one or two toilet necessaries Kate had brought with her for use during her intended stay at Pepo-ni.

The third carried spare ammunition, a trap for catching small game and birds for food, and a few useful medicines—quinine, ipecacuanha, Dover's powder, etc. Uledi carried Gilmour's Express rifle, but otherwise was not burdened, as it was necessary he should not be fatigued nor hampered in his duties as scout and spy. Gilmour himself took his repeating rifle; while each man, in addition to his load, carried forty rounds of ammunition for his Snider, a palm-fibre sleeping-mat, a hunting knife, and salt for his own use. A large pot for general cooking purposes was also taken.

By the time the loads were made up and tied, darkness had come on, and it was useless to think of starting that night. Mr. Kennedy still slept peacefully, and Gilmour took good care he should not be disturbed. After a final look round to see that all was in readiness for an early start next morning, our hero threw himself down on a bench, and, drawing a rug over him, was soon sleeping as soundly as if he had not a care in the world.

At four in the morning, ere yet the first grey streak of dawn had tinged the horizon, Tubu brought a cup of coffee to his master's bedside and softly awoke him. A few minutes later and Gilmour stood ready equipped for his arduous march. Mr. Kennedy was still asleep, and not being desirous of going through any trying farewells, Gilmour refrained from waking him to take leave. Instead, he pencilled a hasty note, and left it to be given to the missionary as soon as he awoke. He briefly described the scheme he had ultimately formed, and spoke cheerfully of his certainty of final success. It might, he said, be some weeks before he could achieve his purpose, as so much depended on how far the Masai had taken Miss Kennedy into their own country before he was able to effect her escape. That he would find means of effecting it he did not doubt; and meantime he (Mr. Kennedy) was to keep up his spirits and give himself a proper chance to recover. "Of one thing be certain," Gilmour concluded; "you shan't see my face again until I bring Miss Kennedy with me."

By the time the letter was finished it was broad daylight, and men and baggage were ready for the road. There stood the select four—Uledi, Tubu, Resasi, and Ferhani—surrounded by their stay-at-home comrades, who bade them good-bye and wished them god-speed with many pious expressions from the Koran.

At length Gilmour emerged from the house and gave his parting injunctions to the men left in charge of the settlement. Then guns were shouldered and loads balanced on the head, and, amid a volley of "Kwahéris" and much pressing of hands, the forlorn hope left the snug quarters of Pepo-ni, and in single file tramped westward through the dew-laden grass and bushes.

In a couple of hours they had reached the plainly discernible track of the Masai, and as nothing was yet to be feared, they pushed along quickly till they crossed the Kikavo river, and found the lately vacated camp.

After a brief halt for rest and refreshment, they once more pushed ahead, Gilmour in too feverish a state of mind to allow of his taking things reasonably. It must be remembered that Gilmour was by no means so sanguine as he had represented to Mr. Kennedy. There was, indeed, some hope in the suggestion he had made, that in all likelihood the Masai would look upon Miss Kennedy as a god ; but, spite of himself, the worst fears *would* force themselves upon him. The extraordinary communities in which the Masai warriors live were only too well known to him, and he found himself giving way to the liveliest apprehensions. His frequent appeals to Uledi only served to intensify his misgivings, that experienced personage drawing the most dreadful and depressing pictures of Masai manners and customs. He did, however, admit the possibility of the bibi's being taken for a lybon, or even for Ngai, but was doubtful how long her captors would remain under that pleasing delusion, especially as Miss Kennedy, in her present position, was bereft of all means of producing an awe-inspiring impression on the native mind.

Besides the horrible fears by which he was haunted, Gilmour was exasperated by the thought that he could not hit upon any feasible scheme of rescue. Even supposing he were in communication with Miss Kennedy now, he had not the vaguest idea how he was to get her out of the hands of her captors. There was nothing for it but to wait and watch; but that was an attitude of inaction which did not suit his boiling temperament, and the sense of helplessness it gave rise to nearly drove him frantic.

Towards evening, after a killing march, the pursuing party reached Kibo-noto. They had now to be more careful in their movements, as they rightly concluded the Masai would almost certainly camp here for the night before entering their own country. Accordingly, they diverged from the plain, and sought refuge in the forest region running along the base of the western slope of Chaga. At a deserted shamba, they found an old hut which was sufficiently habitable, and here they took up their quarters for the night. While one man gathered bananas, which here were to be found in abundance, a second made a fire and prepared to cook some food. Under cover of the growing darkness, the three others ventured down towards the plain, to see whether or not their surmises as to the movements of the Masai had proved correct. Soon the roaring camp-fires were to be seen glowing brightly between the trees and reflecting a ruddy glare on the overhanging clouds. Drawing nearer, Uledi's sharp eye soon detected the little hut Ulu had built for her mistress, and before many moments had passed, Gilmour had the satisfaction of seeing the M-Chaga herself emerge from it. After waiting a little longer in the vain hope of seeing Kate, he turned to go, obliged to be satisfied for that night with the assurance that at least she appeared to be unmolested.

Next day Gilmour was delighted to find that the warriors were making every preparation to remain in camp. It was now time to consider plans. In the first place, it was imperative that either Ulu or Miss Kennedy should be spoken to, so as to find out how they were being treated and let them know that Gilmour was in their immediate vicinity, only awaiting a favourable opportunity to assist them to escape. It would depend on the result of the inquiries as to Kate's treatment whether the projected rescue should be made without delay, or postponed until place and circumstances were more suitable.

The immediate question was how to reach Kate, situated as she now was in the heart of the Masai camp. Nothing seemed feasible but that one of them should enter in the disguise of a Masai; and now came the difficulty—where were they to get the necessary accoutrements?

As Gilmour sat ransacking his brains for a solution of this fresh problem, some one drew his attention to the fact that Uledi had disappeared, leaving

his rifle and all his clothes, with the exception of
his loin-cloth. He had, however, taken the pre-
caution to retain his hunting-knife and revolver.

Gilmour noted these significant details with a
terrible feeling of fear and apprehension. Could
it be possible that his most trusted man had
deserted—the only one, too, who knew Masai-land,
the Masai, and their language as well as he knew
his own country and people? He said nothing to
his other followers; but as hour after hour went
on, and still Uledi did not return, a feeling of deep
despair took possession of him. If Uledi had really
run away, their enterprise was absolutely hopeless.
Distractedly Gilmour kept going in and out of the
hut, and looking about in all directions for some
sign of the fugitive's return.

At length, on one of these occasions, his attention
was arrested by a low, soft whistle, such as his
men were accustomed to use to attract each other's
attention when buffalo-hunting. Gilmour stopped
and listened wonderingly.

"Bwana," softly called a voice from the bush,
"look to your right, but do not shoot."

Gilmour obeyed, and attentively scanned the
undergrowth in the direction indicated. For a
moment he saw nothing extraordinary; then, with
a violent start of sudden alarm, he instinctively
grasped the revolver at his side, as among the

bushes appeared the head and shoulders of a ferociously painted and bedecked Masai warrior. In the shock of the unexpected discovery the warning voice was forgotten, and a bullet would in all probability have abruptly terminated the masquer's brief career, had he not again called out—

"Bwana, Bwana, do not shoot. It is I—Uledi," he added; and out of the bush the trusty fellow stepped, looking as fine a specimen of a Masai warrior as ever brained an M-Swahili or stole his cattle.

For a moment Gilmour stood astounded at the metamorphosis which had taken place in his headman's dress and appearance.

"How did you manage it?" he asked at length.

By way of answer, Uledi drew a blood-stained knife from his rolled-up kid-skin, and proudly held it up for his master's inspection.

"Good God, Uledi!" cried Gilmour. "Have you killed one of them?"

"Yes; and I hope it won't be the last," returned Uledi, coolly wiping the dried blood from the haft of his weapon.

Gilmour shrugged his shoulders. "I suppose this is the sort of thing I must get used to," he said to himself, "if I'm to go in for life and death adventures among savages." Then he turned to Uledi, and asked for fuller details.

At some length Uledi explained how for an hour or two he had watched the Masai camp and awaited his opportunity. His patience was at length rewarded. Observing a Masai wandering at some distance from his comrades, he followed him unnoticed. At the right moment he sprang upon him and seized him by the throat to prevent an outcry. Then, before the warrior had time to recover from the shock, Uledi had stabbed him to death. To strip him and despoil him of his paintbag was the work of a few minutes, to transform himself into his counterpart the work of a few minutes more. The body of the dead Masai being disposed of in a dense piece of bush, Uledi had leisurely retraced his steps, feeling perfectly safe in his disguise and his ability to keep up the character.

That very night the Masai camp was again reconnoitred, but, to Gilmour's intense chagrin, Kate's hut was found to be too well guarded to be approached even under cover of the disguise.

Next day followed the grand orgy which we have already described. A prey to the most painful fears and forebodings, Gilmour viewed the brutal licence of the savage scene from a neighbouring wooded eminence. Hope once more took possession of him, however, as he saw the gorged revellers fall one by one into a condition of stupor, and noted the helpless fashion in which they lay about among the remains of their ghastly banquet.

Safe in the assurance of a careless guard for that night, at least, Uledi approached the camp and, as we have seen, reached Miss Kennedy in safety. When Gilmour, from the tree where he anxiously awaited his headman's return, heard the pistol-shot and saw the hurrying guard, he gave Uledi up for lost. Another hour of uneasiness, however, and Uledi was again beside him, bearer of the joyous tidings that Ulu and the bibi were well and well treated.

Next night, by dint of herculean efforts, the small party contrived to cross the district of Kiraragwa, the western extension of the Njiri plain. At day-break they reached the mountain of Ndapdúk, where they found a place of concealment, whence they could safely watch the arrival of the warriors and note the kraal in which Kate was bestowed.

That night, in spite of blistered feet and stiff joints—the result of their terrible forced march— Gilmour and Uledi descended to the plain. Disguised as hyænas, they approached the kraal and gave the three hoots of an owl, by which signal it had been agreed Kate Kennedy should know her friends were near. Then they returned to their hiding-place to seek forgetfulness of their weariness in sleep.

CHAPTER IX.

ALTHOUGH Gilmour had thus arrived in Miss Kennedy's immediate neighbourhood, he was still as far as ever from the end he had in view. He could devise nothing—think of no practical scheme to effect Kate's rescue. He was quite prepared to risk his life in the attempt, but he had no intention of throwing it away. Besides, death to him meant lifelong imprisonment to the lady. He must see at least a chance of success before he could stake everything on any given venture.

Gilmour's chief difficulty was, not how to get Kate out of the hands of the Masai, but how to get her out of Masai-land. She could not cross the plain in a single night as he had done, nor could they attempt to carry her. At the same time, every other route appeared even more impracticable.

Tossed about between fear and hope, doubt and despair, Gilmour was almost beside himself. In the face of such terrible danger, it was maddening to have to sit still and do nothing. Ever before him floated the image of Miss Kennedy, piteously imploring him to help her, or silently upbraiding him for his inaction. He pictured to himself her surroundings—her disgusting fare, her worse than convict's couch, the evil-smelling hut, and the brutalized men and women who from morning till night crowded about her with their naked, clay-plastered bodies and horrible faces. Then he re-called the refinements of Kate's nature, the graces of her person, her feminine delicacy, and her abhorrence of every form of dirt and nastiness, and thought how all these were being outraged in every particular. The very thought was madness ; and a hundred times a day he cursed what he called his imbecility in being able to form no definite plan of escape. He held long and frequent consultations with Uledi, until even that stoical individual became interested in spite of himself, and, though he could not share his master's eagerness, looked with sym-pathetic eyes on his constant anxiety and unrest. Nevertheless, he had nothing to suggest. Indeed, the whole enterprise appeared to him but an mzungu's mad adventure, for which they would probably all pay with their lives.

Uledi being a fatalist, however, he only shrugged his shoulders expressively, and assiduously set about making his preparations for heaven; that is to say, in accordance with Mohammedan rites, he daily performed an extraordinary number of ablutions, and morning, noon, and night said his prayers with unusual diligence and fervour.

Meanwhile, with a ludicrous expression of sympathy on his ugly face, he patiently humoured his master, and listened gravely to all the latter's impracticable schemes, only to quash them, it must be said, by unanswerable arguments from his own wider experience and fuller knowledge of the Masai and their customs. Still, it was a certain comfort to Gilmour to have some one to talk to from morning till night about the Bibi Kennedy and the manner of her rescue; seeing which, Uledi heard compassionately, inwardly wondering the while why so much fuss should be made about a woman when there were so many in the world. That any man should risk his life for one was a matter passing Uledi's comprehension.

At times even Uledi's society grew irksome, however, and, anxious to be alone with his own thoughts, Gilmour would betake himself to a re-tired though commanding rock, where, heedless of possible sunstrokes, he stretched himself out to focus his glass on the kraal, and patiently watch everything that took place within its precincts, in the hope of catching a glimpse of Kate, or discovering some movement of the Masai by which the escape might be facilitated.

He was lying thus one day, with elbows on the ground, chin resting on his hands, and toes idly kicking the hard rock, when Uledi came to him on some trifling errand or another. Seeing his master's dejection, the man stood wistfully gazing at him for a moment without speaking.

"Ah, Bwana," he said at length, "I think if you had wings you would fly."

"If I were in Ulyiah, I would fly without wings," returned Gilmour moodily.

Uledi looked hurt. "Fly without wings, Bwana! You laugh at me," he said.

"No, Uledi," replied Gilmour, rousing himself, and for the moment forgetting his perplexities in watching the man's half-injured, half-incredulous expression. "I am perfectly serious. In Ulyiah we have carriages that take us through the air faster than a bird can fly."

If Uledi had looked half incredulous before, he looked wholly incredulous now. He said nothing, however, but expectantly awaited the completion of the *lie*.

"Yes," Gilmour went on; "we make a huge bag, shaped like the papaw fruit, and as large as the seyyed's palace at Zanzibar. It is filled with a curious kind of air, and has a little carriage attached.

Then, when the cords by which it is tied to the
earth are let go, it flies upward, and sails on the
wings of the wind to wherever it is wanted."

Uledi tried to look believing, and professed to
appear vastly amazed. It was such a magnificent
lie, this of the Bwana's about the big bag and the
little carriage.

"Allah, what a marvel!" he cried. "Truly
the wazungu have all the secrets of the djins!
Can't you make one here?" he added, referring,
of course, to the flying-machine, or balloon, as we
should simply call it.

"I only wish I could. We should soon carry off
the bibi and Ulu, and if the wind were right, in
two or three hours we might have them at Mombasa,
or even Zanzibar."

The rapturous grin on Uledi's face broadened.
The invention was really superb; and with all his
soul the man envied his master's gift of lying—an
accomplishment much coveted and greatly culti-
vated among the Wa-Swahili. It was, indeed, one
of the great grievances among Gilmour's men that
the Bwana would not exercise his power in the
more ordinary affairs of life, when he had so many
opportunities of using it to advantage.

Already Gilmour had turned his eyes to the
plain below again. "Oh, Uledi," he cried, "can't
you think of anything?"

But Uledi was still without resources. "Please God, something will turn up," was all he said, as he went off to rejoin his comrades, and repeat, with additions, the Bwana's latest display of inventive genius.

Gilmour, once more left to himself, returned to his scrutiny of the kraal and to his thoughts of the English girl, who, for the present, was doomed to share its miseries.

One day passed much the same as another on the heights of Ndapdúk. Unless some trivial little incident or brief snatch of conversation, such as that we have described, nothing ever occurred to break the weary monotony of watching and waiting. Every night Gilmour ventured down to the plain in his usual disguise, and crawled with Uledi to a large tree near the kraal, where he derived a certain dismal satisfaction in sounding the melancholy notes which served as a signal between himself and Kate.

The kraal being occupied by el-morúū, it was protected by a stout thorn fence, in which there was a single gateway, kept carefully closed all night. In vain, in their character of hyænas, and imitating the ungainly movements of these brutes, Gilmour and Uledi sniffed and peered about. Not a hole or gap was to be found, and, after running imminent risk of discovery through the furious

barking of the pariah dogs, there was nothing for
it but to return, wearied and disheartened, to the
mountain.

There was one result of all this ceaseless thinking about Miss Kennedy of which Gilmour was as
yet unconscious. He became as much absorbed
in dwelling on the manifold excellences of her
character and person as in the question of her
rescue. He was always telling himself what a remarkable girl she was—a girl who appealed to a
" fellow's head and heart—none of your simpering
boarding-school misses," and so forth. Of course,
he never for a moment imagined that he was falling
in love with her. The love illusion, like so many
others, was dissipated for ever. Bachelorhood,
he had vowed to himself a hundred times, hence-
forth would be his fate. And yet, in spite of this
forlorn and melancholy conclusion, Kate's image
continued more and more to usurp the place ever
held by *that other*, until his "intense interest" in
Kate held as complete sway over Gilmour's day
and night dreams as his "love" for the other had
done in earlier days.

Strange perhaps to say, this feeling grew and
flourished on an empty stomach and a daily
tightening belt. Not having been able to use their
guns, and their little store of European articles
being rigorously kept for Kate, the rescue party

had to depend upon what they could get by trap and arrow, which was not only marvellously little, but mighty tough and unsavoury. To make matters worse, they were in continual danger of being discovered by the Masai herdsmen, who were encroaching more and more upon the mountain pasturages as the dry season advanced. Another disquieting circumstance was the non-appearance of Ulu. "Could it be," Gilmour more than once asked himself, "that Ulu had sunk back into her old savage life, and preferred to remain where she was? Might she not have betrayed them? Pooh! What nonsense! If she had done so, they would have been hunted for long ago. No, no; little Ulu would never do that!"

Still her non-appearance was a worrying source of inquietude. Situated as Gilmour and his men were, it was difficult to maintain an attitude of patient waiting on Providence, though, Micawber-like, they daily hoped something favourable would turn up.

At length Gilmour's suspense was brought to an end.

One day, as he lay on his favourite rock watching the kraal, he was startled by the movement of some branches in the neighbourhood. Instinctively he dropped behind a boulder, and then, with revolver ready, waited to see who or what would appear.

He was not kept long in suspense. The bushes moved, some branches were pushed aside, and out popped the head of a Masai maiden, eagerly peering round as if in search of something.

By good luck Gilmour noted the age and sex of the individual in time to repress his first impulse to fire. He found himself, however, in a painful quandary. To allow that girl to advance and discover their hiding-place would be absolutely disastrous to their projects.

For a moment he asked himself, What was the death of a Masai *ditto* as compared with the life and freedom of Miss Kennedy? His fingers twitched nervously over the trigger. A little more of the same almost involuntary movement, and the girl's life would have been at an end. Happily he mastered his terrible desire to fire, as he thought that there would at least be no harm in waiting to see if she was alone.

Cautiously the girl advanced in the direction of the improvised hut. Evidently there was no one with her. Gilmour, noting that fact, resolved to capture her. Taking advantage of her back being turned towards him, he emerged from behind the boulder, and with catlike steps followed. The distance between them was noiselessly lessened, and all-unconsciously the girl stole onward, too absorbed in her search to hear or see anything behind. At length Gilmour was close to her. With a sudden movement he grasped hold of her shrinking form, and in a trice one hand was over her mouth and an arm round her, pinioning her as in a vice.

With all the vigour and suppleness of a cat, the girl writhed and struggled. In her convulsive movements, to which fear of death gave extraordinary strength, she contrived to get her face turned toward her captor. In an instant the horrified expression of her face changed. She remained quiescent, though she tried to speak.

Gilmour, thinking he was suffocating her, removed his hand from off her mouth.

" Bwana, Bwan' mkubwa ! " the girl gasped out.

With an exclamation Gilmour let her go. "Good heavens, Ulu! is it you?" he cried in amazement, as she fell to the ground, panting and exhausted by her fierce fight for life; and hardly believing his eyes, Gilmour surveyed her almost unrecognizable figure, and tried to realize that this was indeed the girl he had been educating to make his wife.

Her face was thickly plastered with clay and oil, and her formerly dainty dress, coloured by the same materials, was not to be distinguished from the bullock-hides which clothed the persons of Masai women.

Ulu, remarking his astonishment, became sud-

denly aware of her terrible backsliding into the
dear, delicious ways of her "days of ignorance,"
and lay terribly abashed, fearing some outbreak of
wrath from her lord and master.

But whatever reflections may have transiently
crossed Gilmour's mind, he gave them no expression. On recovering from his surprise, his first
thought was of Kate, and he poured an eager flood
of questions upon Ulu regarding the welfare of her
mistress. Was she well? How were the Masai
treating her? What was she doing? How was
she living?

"The bibi is well," Ulu stammered out, hardly
yet recovered from her fright. "She sends you
her salaams and compliments."

"Yes, yes! What else?" queried Gilmour,
eagerly.

"The bibi looks continually towards the mountain," the girl continued. "She awaits your
coming."

"Would to God I knew what to do!" groaned
Gilmour inwardly. "Have you no other news?"
he went on, addressing his companion. "Don't
you know what they are going to do with
her?"

"Oh yes," replied Ulu. "The el-moran and
the el-morūū have consulted Mbaratian" (the
great lybon or medicine man of the Masai). "He

says she must be taken further into the country—towards Naivasha, I think."

This terrible news fell like lead upon Gilmour's heart, and he could only reply with a scared look. If once Miss Kennedy was taken so far from Kilimanjaro, then adieu to all hopes of rescue.

"Do you know when she is to go?" he asked, recovering himself with an effort.

"Bwana, I know not. Probably not for several days, as the warriors who are to escort her must go to the woods to eat meat."

Gilmour uttered an exclamation of relief, as if some little ray of hope lay in this last piece of intelligence. Then, with impatient energy, he added, "Come, let us seek Uledi."

The new position of affairs having been detailed to the assembled Zanzibaris, Gilmour asked their advice.

"We must rescue her at once," was Uledi's sententious remark.

"Bless my soul, of course we must rescue her!" cried his master fiercely. "But how? how? how?" and with baffled look and hands crammed in his pockets, he stamped about in feverish excitement.

Uledi had no answer ready, and could only mutter something about the pleasure of Allah, and chaw his tooth-stick meditatively.

"By Jove, I have it!" cried Gilmour suddenly, stopping short in his walking. "I see how it may be done now. We must find out a new place of concealment on Dónyo Erók there"—he went on, pointing to a neighbouring mountain to the east. "That arranged, we must devise some awe-inspiring means for effecting the escape of the bibi, so as to make the Masai imagine she has gone off by her own miraculous power. We shall then all take refuge during the night at the new hiding-place, and there lie hid for some days, till we are sure there is no pursuit, after which we may find a way to cross the plain to Kilimanjaro. There! What do you think of that, Uledi?" and Gilmour turned half joyfully, half imploringly towards his headman.

"Your scheme is very risky," commenced Uledi, doubtfully; then more resignedly, "But if it is the will of Allah, we will rescue the bibi as you suggest."

"Then, let us set to work at once," cried Gilmour, delighted beyond measure at having got a plan at last. "Ulu, can you get back to-day with the news?"

"If the Bwana wills it I shall return. But the people of our kraal think I have gone to visit a distant relative, and do not expect me till to-morrow."

"Oh, then of course you must stop here to-night.

Now, Ferhani," Gilmour continued, "you know something about Dónyo Erók. You had better come with me to-night to look out for our new hiding-place."

"No, no, Bwana!" burst in energetic chorus from all the men. "Your life is very precious; ours are those of dogs. Some of us will go."

Eventually Gilmour gave in, and allowed Ferhani and Tubu to take the dangerous task in hand.

The night was spent with Uledi and Ulu in sanguine discussion of the means by which the rescue was to be effected, varied by eager questions as to how the bibi endured this and how adapted herself to that. Gilmour also got time to read Ulu a mild rebuke, but was prepared to overlook matters a hundred times worse in consideration of her devotion to Miss Kennedy. Indeed he could have felt it in his heart to have given her a good hug, even as she was, so grateful was he for all her loving and faithful service.

In the morning Ulu returned, bearing with her a note for the bibi, and having made an arrangement to come every morning to the tree near the kraal, in a rift of which she would find a note to warn them when the moment for action had arrived.

CHAPTER X.

WHILE Gilmour thus schemed and fumed in his concealment on the heights of Ndapdúk, Miss Kennedy's position at the base of the mountain was by no means an enviable one.

To acquire a proper idea of her surroundings, let the reader imagine a circular tunnel formed of interlaced sticks, four feet high and from five to six feet broad, the roof being only slightly curved. Further imagine this tunnel of wicker-work partitioned off into some hundred cells, each eight feet long, and having a hole which did duty as a doorway towards the inner aspect of the circle. Such was the general aspect of the kraal in which Kate was confined. Outside this continuous line of huts a strong thorn fence gave protection against man and beast, while inside, in the large open space, eighty yards in diameter, the herds and flocks of the inhabitants were secured each night.

As the kraal had only recently been built—the

Masai being migratory in their habits—the place was fairly habitable, its sanitary condition being improved by the hot sun and drying winds which then prevailed.

In the wet season things are sadly different. To keep out the heavy rains the huts are plastered thickly with dung, over which dressed hides are tied or loaded down with stones to prevent their being blown off by the wind. It requires no great stretch of the imagination to realize that the huts thus protected become excessively odorous, and harbour a myriad vermin of a troublesome character. Outside, matters are even worse, for the space occupied by the cattle becomes one gigantic cesspool and reeking dung-hill, where during the day clouds of flies find congenial haunts, forming a pest not second, even to the mosquitoes of the marshes of the coast lowlands, to such travellers as have not hides proof against their irritating attacks.

To add to the amenities of Kate's position, she was given a large new hut somewhat apart from the rest, and having a little courtyard of its own, specially fenced off for the reception of the calves, which as yet had not arrived.

At dawn on the morning following her arrival at Ndapdúk, Miss Kennedy awoke with a start, not quite sure whether she was dreaming or waking.

A strange, unearthly chorus of noises sounded through the chill damp air. The light was only beginning to steal faintly through the interstices of the wicker-work. Bewildered, Kate rubbed her eyes, but could see nothing. Still at intervals to her ears were wafted the unearthly sounds, coming ever nearer, rising ever more shrilly and strangely. That she was not asleep, however, became evident when Ulu, waking up, rose and pushed aside the hide which did duty as a door. With the inrush of cold air came an intensified volume of sound.

"Come, Bibi, come outside; the women await you," cried Ulu, at the same time creeping out herself.

Kate shuddered. "More horrid sights!" she exclaimed. "When will this end, I wonder?" But there was no help for it—she must place herself once more on exhibition. Her wisest plan, she recognized, was to humour her captors in the absurd fancies they cherished regarding her. Plucking up courage as Ulu again called her, she wrapped a kaross of monkey-skins about her, and stepped out of the hut.

A strange sight met her eyes, made doubly strange by the grey obscurity of early dawn. In the centre of the kraal all the women and girls of the neighbourhood were assembled. They presented a very ghastly appearance, their faces being

painted with a band of white curving on each side
from the forehead round the temple to the cheek-
bone. Their heads, bare and clean shaved, glistened
with oil, and all were adorned in their best, in
beads, iron wire, and hides.

This witchlike assembly, on seeing Kate emerge
from her hut, broke off their chant and burst into
a shrill, trilling cry of salutation. The greeting
over, a withered old dame quavered out in a weak
broken voice what we may have the gallantry to
call a song, to which the rest of the women kept
time with a curious mincing step, and at intervals
a general shaking up of the body, as they moved
slowly towards Kate. At the close of each stanza
they all stood still and raised their cracked voices
in chorus.

In this manner they gradually approached her
to whom they looked as their deity, till at length
they formed a circle round her, within which the
leading beldame moved about as if intoxicated or
in the last stage of idiocy. The song now rose
shriller than ever, as they dipped tufts of grass
into calabashes of milk which they carried, and
held them out dripping towards Kate. Thus employed with voice and hand, the uncouth worshippers slowly moved round in a ring, stamping
their feet as they went, so as to cause the little
iron bells on their ankles to tinkle. The evolution

was one not to be accomplished without pain. Every now and then one or other of the crowd might be seen stooping to twist round the heavy iron casings of her legs, as if they chafed raw sores, the common consequence among Masai women of their martyr-like adherence to fashion.

Of the meaning of this demonstration Kate could form only the haziest idea. For a time she stood bewildered. Gradually, however, it dawned upon her that she was being invoked for some special purpose. "Poor creatures! They must be praying for my blessing on their grass and on their cattle," she concluded, and for the moment her natural enough repulsion at the women's degradation was lost in pity of their ignorance and misery.

Having continued to circle round for some time, the women proceeded to pass in line before Kate, depositing the grass in a heap at her feet, and emptying the milk upon it. Then they stood silent, seemingly expectant of some favour.

Were they waiting for some special manifestations of her supposed supernatural powers? Kate asked herself with inward misgiving. What was she to do? She looked towards Ulu as a probable source of inspiration, but Ulu was nowhere to be seen. For a moment she stood irresolute, unable to think of any way out of the difficulty, yet dreading the consequences of her inaction. Suddenly

she remembered the peculiar Masai form of bene-
diction, and stepping up to the grass she spat upon
it vigorously and perhaps just a little vindictively.
With delighted screams, the women immediately
rushed forward in a scrambling mass to secure
a little of the grass so blessed; and while they
worried like dogs, scratching, pulling, striking,
screaming over it, Kate turned away and sought
refuge in her hut, where for a time she was left
in peace.

As the sun appeared on the horizon the final
celebration and closing acts of the successful expedition commenced. With almost every other purely
African race these would have taken the form of
a grand pombé-drinking and ngomma, such as has
already been described in an earlier chapter. Not
so with the Masai. Singing and dancing as an
enjoyment in themselves are unknown among these
strange people. Song is only employed as a means
of invoking the aid of Ngai, or of celebrating a
victorious raid, while the dance is indulged in
solely by the women as part of their religious rites.
Musical instruments, likewise, are unknown, not
even a drum being found throughout the length
and breadth of Masai-land. Again, beer and other
intoxicating liquors are only rarely partaken of by
the el-morūū, or married men, the diet of the
warriors being strictly confined to the flesh of

domestic animals and milk; to taste any other food would be to lose caste and be disgraced. Hence the only forms of enjoyment left open to the Masai are gorging themselves with meat, holding long-winded but admirably conducted debates, and gratifying their passion for the fierce delights of battle and cattle-lifting. To these may be added various military displays in which they indulge on important occasions.

It was one of these last exhibitions which the el-moran now commenced, before the division of the spoil and the final break-up of the army. A chanted recitative, accompanied by a chorus such as they had raised on reaching Kiraragwa, broke the morning stillness, sonorously howled forth by some hundreds of warriors who had collected outside the kraal.

Kate, on hearing the song of victory, guessed that some new torture was in store for her, and shrank more than ever from showing herself. Ulu, however, declared that she must humour the el-moran on this their final day in camp. Afterwards she would probably be left in peace to the guardianship of the elders, who would treat her with due respect. Again Kate yielded to the stern logic of facts, and, taking Ulu by the hand, ventured forth.

This time it was necessary to go outside the kraal. The women, some of the older men, and the children escorted her to the tree from which Gilmour had signalled, and there under the shady branches she was soon installed. The el-moran, in all the terror of war array, exhibited their military skill in various simple evolutions of such a nature as showed they had learned the value of discipline and united action. Now they advanced in line in one direction, suddenly to fall into single file and move at right angles. Next they dropped into some half-dozen lines, the alternate ones going in contrary directions, so that, moving in a maze among themselves, they produced a bewildering appearance as their bright shovel-headed spears glittered in the sun. At a given signal they scattered as if to hide behind bushes, or gathered to dash forward in an irresistible rush.

This display over, they formed up in line again and stood at ease. Resting the points of their shields on the ground, and leaning partly on them, partly on their spears, they commenced once more to sing—whether something in their own glorification, or a prayer to Ngai, Kate could not say. Their facial contortions in this exercise were ludicrous to behold. No note was dragged out without a determined and seemingly painful struggle, to judge from the manner in which their necks were twisted, mouths screwed awry, and eyes appealingly uplifted till only the whites were visible.

The warlike display was now brought to an end by a performance which might variously be described as a game, a dance, or simply a gymnastic feat. The warriors still singing, one of their number left the ranks and hopped like a bird in front of his comrades. Here, with a face of portentous solemnity, and with his arms closely pressed to his side, he commenced to leap straight up in the air, but *without bending his legs* to take the spring. The difficulty of doing this till essayed is not obvious. The height and number of times the leaper can attain is the aim in this characteristic feat of Masai athletics.

The more serious work of the day had now to be set about. The cattle still remained undivided, and the women and boys looked forward with joyous excitement to some bloodshed over this usually ticklish business. Rarely did a raid end without the death of several warriors in the fighting which commonly marked the division of the spoil. Not unfrequently, indeed, more men were killed on these occasions than during the raid itself; the simple rule being recognized—

> " That he may take who has the power,
> And he may keep who can.

In consequence, the weak, the timid, and the very young had usually to be content with the glory of the capture, and with little that was substantial, except what might be contemptuously left to them of the lean and sickly among the cattle.

The herd was now driven up to the kraal, and a pretty fair division made, the cattle being allotted to the various sections of the army according to the number of warriors each contained. A vast amount of angry shouting and disputing, with some threatening movements, marked this primary division, but beyond that nothing happened, to the visible chagrin of the women who appeared to be disappointed that matters did not come to a bloodier issue.

Those sections of the army which came from a distance drove their shares a little way off, and afterwards gathered round to see if there would be any fighting over the final division of the spoil which remained to the warriors of Ndapdúk.

The young women were especially forward in making remarks tending to raise a row. They hounded on their sweethearts to show their bravery and prowess by seizing the lion's share. The warriors, excited by the bloodthirsty cries, watched each other's movements like dogs as they stood in a circle round the frightened cattle. At length, amid renewed clamour, the lytunu and the lygonani of the section strode forth like men to whom none would dare say nay. From the herd they separated so many cattle and drove them to their friends to guard. This much was conceded to them as their right; if they wanted more they must take their chance in the general scramble.

The advance of the leaders a second time was the signal for a general eager rush upon the herd. With shouts and blows, each man selected particular cattle, and in feverish haste drove them, bewildered and half-mad, to the custody of ready hands among the onlookers. The spoil being large and the party comparatively small, even the more timid secured a share.

But the tug of war was yet to come. Amid immense excitement, the warriors hurried back, each one bent on making the most of his opportunities. Some of the more ruthless and reckless, with threatening scowl and gesture, caused the less hardy to give up their timidly asserted claims; the result being that a few retired from the *mêlée* empty-handed, amid the jeers of the onlookers.

For a time it seemed as if there would be no fight, to the acute disappointment and disgust of all concerned. Such a tame ending to the day's proceedings would be a disgrace to the tribe. Accordingly, the few bullies and hardy spirits who still disputed possession of particular cattle were encouraged by their respective friends to hold out. In several cases this had the desired effect, and, to the delight of the crowd, the arbitrament of battle was decided upon.

Amid a deafening uproar the ground was cleared for the fights. The men were known as the bravest of the Elgéji-Masai, and life and death struggles were anticipated. The disputing parties were taken by pairs, so as to lengthen out the enjoyment of the occasion. With the *sang-froid* proper to men to whom battle was the dearest pleasure in life, they set themselves to examine their arms. Their war adornments were laid aside, as being only of use in frightening Wa-nyika and other "old women."

The canine clamour of the onlookers was hushed as Kombo and Simba, two of their most renowned warriors, stepped into the arena. They took their places a few paces apart, holding their shields before their bodies in such a manner as to leave only the head exposed. For a moment they eyed one another critically, each taking the measure of his man and forming his plan of attack and defence.

Amid profound silence, the two el-moran at length slowly began to move forward, their bodies bent panther-like, ready to spring. A few steps and they were within striking distance. But they were in no hurry to commence. For a time they were content to dodge about, awaiting their opportunity. Apparently they were equally matched; no advance was made or bold stroke given. This, however, did not suit the crowd. Becoming impatient to see blood, they raised derisive cries and mocking laughs. Ironically the *dittoes* (young women) asked to be allowed to do the fighting, declaring that the men were no better than Lajomba. Thus ridiculed, the combatants became infuriated, more reckless in thrust, less careful in defence. The interest rose proportionately, and encouraging shouts goaded them on to bolder deeds. Delighted applause greeted the infliction of some flesh-wounds. Blood at last was beginning to flow.

Still no decided advantage was gained on either side, though now the fight had raged for some time, and the combatants panted with their exertions. At length Kombo essayed the hazard of a dangerous stroke, one that few dared try. Awaiting his opportunity, he gathered himself together with a mighty effort, and rapidly aiming for Simba's head, he drove his spear at the almost impenetrable leather of his shield. The stroke was magnificently given. Through the shield clove the spear. Back staggered Simba. His shield was driven against him, apparently nailed to his skull. As he dropped on his knee a roar of applause burst from every onlooker. But the warrior only staggered for a moment, stunned, not dead. The spear in cleaving the leather had slightly deflected, and instead of splitting his skull it had merely glanced along the bone, exposing it and cutting off an ear.

As Simba sprang to his feet, to the surprise of all, he was received with a shout equal to that which a moment before had greeted his opponent. It was now Kombo who was in a desperate plight. He had played his best, almost his only, card. It had failed, and he was now in an infinitely worse position than before, for so deeply was the spear embedded in the thick, tough hide that it could not be withdrawn. With the fury of despair, Kombo tried to withdraw it, but to do so he had to run *backwards*. To prevent this, Simba, his gashed head all bloody and hideous, followed up, pushing the shield as hard as the other pulled the spear. Naturally in such an unequal race the odds were against Kombo. At any moment he might trip, or in watching his footsteps receive a thrust from Simba's spear.

Kombo, finding his efforts in vain, suddenly changed his tactics. Putting forth all his strength, he gave a tremendous tug and as suddenly let go. Simba, thus taken unawares, stumbled forward, temporarily exposing himself. Quick as lightning, Kombo's knobkerry was whirled, with all the concentrated fury of one who fights for life and honour, at the exposed head of his enemy. The gods, however, were against him, for the club

caught the edge of Simba's slanting shield, and,
thus deflected, went flying harmless overhead.

Kombo was now both spearless and clubless.
He had but to prepare to die. He scorned to
ask for quarter. He would die as became a Masai
warrior, fighting to the last. With clenched teeth,
starting eyeballs, and breath coming hard and fast,
he once more seized his embedded spear, while the
air rang with the admiring plaudits of the throng
that surged in irrepressible excitement around the
combatants.

Simba was rapidly becoming weak from loss of
blood. There was, therefore, a chance for Kombo,
if he could but hold out long enough. This the
former recognized, for, with desperate fury, he
pushed back his opponent, making at the same
time furious lunges with his spear. The end,
however, came at last. Kombo, running backward,
struck his foot against a stone and overbalanced
himself. As he fell on his back, Simba's spear
descended upon him with a horrible stroke, and
pinned him to the ground. There, as he lay
twisting in the agonies of death, the victor fell
fainting on the top of him.

The next dispute was settled in an equally blood-
thirsty manner. It closed, however, more speedily.
The spear-handle of one of the combatants broke.
His opponent, prematurely raising a cry of triumph,

jumped forward to take advantage of the accident. But the other was even more quick to seize an opportunity, and ere the confident shout was half uttered, it was ended abruptly, as a club drove like a bolt from a catapult against his skull, braining him on the spot.

The other cases were finished after a similar fashion, and by sunset half a dozen corpses testified how the Masai arranged cattle-disputes. The victors were received as heroes, and the vanquished, looked upon as so much carrion, were dragged into the bush, round which gathered in gross conclave vultures and marabout storks. Later on, in the murky gloom of night, the hyænas rendered a ghoulish assistance, snarling and laughing in horribly human-like manner as they tore the bodies to pieces, till the morning sun shone upon a few bloody bones and ghastly skulls, sole remains of the lusty warriors of the previous day.

CHAPTER XI.

It must not be supposed that Miss Kennedy was a spectator of the bloodthirsty fights we have just described. She had seen the first furious scramble for the cattle ; but, luckily, in the eager excitement which ensued over the gladiator-like combats, she was forgotten, and left free to follow her own devices. Even Ulu had deserted her, fascinated by the horror of the thrilling scenes.

Thus left to herself outside the screaming circle of onlookers, Kate at first did not move, afraid lest she should attract attention. At length, when the excitement was nearing fever pitch, she slipped quietly to the gate, and, unobserved, sought refuge in her hut.

A considerable flutter ensued when, the disputes finally settled, it was remarked that Ngai was nowhere to be seen. The discovery that Kate was still within the kraal, however, caused the panic which threatened, to subside at once, and the warriors and elders withdrew to consider in conclave what was to be done with their captive. Some held that she—or, as they styled her, he—should be carried farther north; others, that she should remain where she was. The el-moran eloquently stated their claim to have Ngai in their keeping and in their kraals, that they might become more bold in battle and more successful in cattle-lifting. The el-morūū were equally urgent in asserting their fitness as men of wisdom and counsel to have the god in their keeping, adding that it was more important to their existence as a people that families should increase and multiply, and that there should be plenty of grass for their cattle, and abundance of meat and milk for themselves.

The discussion continued till sunset, when it was finally agreed to refer the matter to their great lybon, Mbaratian, when they took him his customary share of the spoil. In pursuance of this mission, a party of warriors and elders started next day for Nguruma, the home of the medicine man for the time being.

In the days which elapsed before the return of the messengers, Kate was little troubled except by the elders, who in the cool evenings delighted to gather round her, and feast their eyes upon her with undiminished wonder. Usually they were silent, but sometimes curiosity prompted them to ask questions of Ulu, who was ever only too ready to answer them in her own peculiar way. The position of interpreter suited the little M-Chaga immensely. Her imagination, though crude, was exuberant, and she possessed in no small degree the faculty of lying, so highly coveted by her race. Nothing pleased her better than to cram her audience with all sorts of astounding stories about Ngai and his wonderful powers. She kept up the mystery that hung about Kate's peculiar shape, making the simple folks believe that her dress was part of herself and grew with her, but that certain portions—her boots, for example—could be taken off and put on at will. Under this skilful treatment it was little wonder that Kate's supernatural reputation grew and flourished, the awe it inspired fortunately exempting it from being put to any severe test.

In no case did her worshippers become obtrusive or too inquisitive, and Kate gradually became accustomed to being perpetually gazed at from a respectful distance whenever she showed herself out of doors. It was, indeed, her only source of amusement to watch the varying expression on the men's tell-tale faces, and note the naïve simplicity of their ideas as far as these could be gathered from their looks.

When alone, Kate's thoughts turned incessantly towards Gilmour. He was her one comfort, her one hope. She herself could think of no means of escape from imprisonment, and, strong and self-reliant as she had ever been, the sense of her present utter helplessness constantly recurred to weigh her down. Then, when her despondency was at its worst, her mind unconsciously would turn to Gilmour, and at once the outlook grew more hopeful. She had the utmost confidence in him, and relied on him implicitly, sure that he would find a way of rescue, even though she herself saw none.

By what curious instinct Kate invariably arrived at this conclusion it would be difficult to tell. She herself puzzled over the matter a good deal in those long, weary days of captivity—the feeling from which it seemed to spring was so new, so unreasonable, as she often told herself. She scarcely knew Mr. Gilmour at all, she said; it was not so very long since he had been to her "the mystery of Chaga." She was not sure, indeed, that he was not now more of a " mystery " to her than ever—there was such disparity between his present manner of life and his natural tastes and sympathies, such as these were by her conceived. Then Kate would rehearse her various theories to account for this disparity, and go over all the little discoveries she had made that seemed to justify her in regarding Gilmour, as she wished to regard him, as the bravest, most noble, most generous of men.

Of course Kate idealized. What woman under the circumstances would not have idealized? Every idol is supposed to have a prejudice in favour of its own peculiar set of worshippers, an anthropomorphic conception of the ways of deity which is based on universal, human experience. Who could blame Kate, then, if, when she thought of all Gilmour had done and was still doing for her, of all he had risked and all he must yet risk—who could blame her if she saw in him excellences of character hitherto undetected, and ascribed to him virtues he did not possess, or even pretend to?

Apart though they were, the thoughts both of Kate and of Gilmour were thus continually running on very much the same lines. Both awaited with impatience the hour of rescue; both continually wondered by what means Kate's escape was to be effected. Each thought the other the most interesting and likeable person he or she had ever met; each justified that conclusion by reference to numerous mental and moral qualities of unusual excellence.

Needless to say, it was all and only friendship. His past, bitter disappointment had long ago led Gilmour to accept the fate of prospective bachelor-

hood, to which he constantly consigned himself, as
a matter of course. Kate, on her part, was a bit of
a cynic on the subject of love, and had early
determined to keep herself free of its fetters. Like
Beatrice, she looked upon all men as her brothers,
and—well, if she favoured one " brother " more
than another, where was the harm or danger in
that ?

There was one question which continually came
athwart all Kate's more pleasing hopes and speculations, and, spite of her faith in her daily more
trusted friend, filled her mind with ever-increasing
anxiety. What would become of her if Mbaratian
decreed that she should be taken further into the
Masai country ? Gilmour did not know the new
danger which threatened her, and every attempt
Kate made to communicate with him through Ulu
had in one way or other been frustrated.

At length the messengers returned, and before
many minutes were over Kate knew her doom.
She was to be conveyed to Naivasha, as soon as a
fitting escort could be got in readiness. As Kate
listened, a cold feeling of despair crept into her
heart. If she could only let Gilmour know, surely
he would make some attempt, however desperate,
to rescue her, rather than that she should be consigned to a life worse than death in the heart of
Masai-land ?

She held a long consultation with Ulu, who hit upon the plan of making capital out of their approaching departure, and, devising the excuse of going to visit a relative, succeeded in reaching Gilmour in the manner already described. Left alone for the night, for the first time Kate realized how much she leaned upon Ulu, and what a feeling of protection and companionship there was in the girl's mere presence. She dared not allow herself to sleep, fearful lest some new danger should come upon her unawares. Slowly the weary hours crept on, seeming as if they would never pass. Once or twice Kate nodded drowsily, always to start up again in sudden affright lest the darkness should conceal some lurking foe.

Daybreak came at last, and with it a feeling of greater assurance. The morning passed uneventfully enough, and at midday Ulu returned, bringing with her a note from Gilmour and the good news that an attempt at rescue was speedily to be made. The note was scribbled on a leaf from Gilmour's pocket diary, and was commonplace enough; but Kate read it as if each word were inspired.

"DEAR MISS KENNEDY" (it ran),

"Keep up your courage. We have at length devised a plan to get you out of the hands of the Philistines in a sufficiently awe-inspiring manner. We cannot be ready for at least three days, however, and after that it may be necessary to wait a day or two longer to be sure of a night when there are no el-moran in the kraal. We shall look to you to let us know when circumstances are favourable. A white handkerchief tied to the roof of your hut will serve as a signal. That night we shall shake hands again, and you will be in safety as far as stout hearts and good guns can assure you of it. Till we meet

" Sincerely yours,

" Tom L. Gilmour."

The reading of this very practical epistle finished, Kate listened with a full heart to Ulu's recital of all that had taken place during her visit to the mountain, and overwhelmed the little girl with questions regarding the nature of Gilmour's present situation and surroundings. To Ulu, accustomed to the hardship and privation of a savage life, there was nothing very remarkable in the position of the rescue party beyond the shortness of the commons. She certainly did think they were very badly fed. But to Kate, the dangers of their hiding-place and the semi-starvation they had to undergo assumed appalling proportions, which the recollection that it was all undertaken and cheerfully accepted on her account served not a little to enhance. Gratitude seemed a poor word to express the feeling which filled her heart and brought the tears to her eyes when she thought of Gilmour and all he had done and dared for her.

What the result of the new venture would be Kate scarcely took time to ask. Again and again she read Gilmour's letter, each fresh perusal giving her new heart, until at length doubt seemed to be forgotten, and already she saw herself safe under the protection of him whom even now she delighted to call her preserver.

"So he is called 'Tom,' is he?" she mused, laying down the letter, after going through it for the twentieth time. "Not much of a name, certainly; but short and convenient enough, at any rate. There's a good, honest sound about it too. What will the 'L' stand for now, I wonder?" and Kate puckered her brow and looked meditative, as if the question were one of the highest importance and must be decided at once. Then she bethought herself that the letter must be answered. "Ulu," she said, holding up Gilmour's note, "I want to send a paper like this to the Bwana. How do you think we can manage it?"

"Quite easily, bibi. I will take it to the tree where he comes every night, and leave it there. He will be sure to find it."

"Of course. How stupid of me not to think of

that before!" and Kate jumped up as if to go in
search of her writing materials. Then she remembered that she had none, and her bright, happy
expression changed to one of extreme vexation.
"If only Mr. Gilmour hadn't written on both sides
of the sheet!" she exclaimed, her eyes wandering
around the hut, as if possibly they might light on
something that might do as a substitute for paper.
They fell upon her saddle-bags. "Oh, I know!"
she cried joyously; and, laying hold of the bags, in
a few moments she had their contents on the
ground, and had found the object she was in
search of. It was a small volume of Browning,
one she had been taking with her to Pepo-ni to
show Gilmour some of her favourite passages, and
claim his sympathy in those yearnings after the
ideal which were to Kate as the expression of her
own deepest longings.

Almost with a pang at the necessary mutilation,
Kate tore out the fly-leaf, and then found herself
confronted by a new difficulty. She had neither
pencil nor pen and ink. Once more she appealed
to Ulu.

"Oh, mtoto, what shall I do?" she cried. "I
have nothing to—to—nothing to make marks with
on this bit of paper;" and she turned a perplexed
face towards her attentive handmaiden, who had
been watching Kate's movements with interest,

wondering what new piece of magic she was about to see performed. " I want to speak to the Bwana," Kate went on, in answer to Ulu's look of astonished inquiry. " White people can speak to each other even at a distance, you know, if only they have paper and something to make marks with like these;" and she indicated the writing in Gilmour's note, the meaning of which Ulu had been utterly at a loss to understand. "All white people know at once what the marks mean, whenever they see them."

Ulu could not make it out; but one thing she grasped clearly enough—the bibi wanted something to make marks with.

"Wait, bibi," she said; " I think I can get you something;" and she quitted the hut, and ran off towards the kraal. "There! will that do?" she asked, returning in a minute or two, triumphantly carrying a tiny skin-bag of paint.

"The very thing!" exclaimed Kate, joyfully. " Now, mtoto, bring me some straw."

Ulu did as desired, and from among the coarse, stiff stems Kate selected one, and with her pen-knife fashioned it into a pen.

"Now for the paint-bag!" she cried; and, squatting on the ground, with the open Browning on her knee for a desk, Kate dipped her pen in the paint, and gravely set herself to write.

" D," she commenced in the extreme left-hand corner of her paper. There was no visible result. She tried again. There was still no answering sign. "Oh, bother! the thing won't write," she exclaimed in a tone of vexation, narrowly examining the point of her impromptu pen.

Kate could see nothing to amend, however, and with another fierce little dip in the paint, she once more essayed to write.

"D . . ." It was no use; the paint was too oily. Kate could produce nothing legible. "I don't care; I'll manage it somehow," she cried hotly, and, with a look of determination, she pulled up the sleeve of her dress, so as to expose her arm.

" What is it you want, bibi ?" asked Ulu, puzzled what to make of her mistress's movement.

" Blood," was the laconic response.

" Then, take mine;" and Ulu offered her arm, thinking from Kate's impetuous energy that some quantity might be required.

"Thank you, mtoto, but I mean to have my own;" and, opening her knife, Kate made a vicious little dab at her wrist with the sharp point of the blade.

Shedding one's own blood is not so easy as might be imagined, and it was not until after one or two unsuccessful attempts that Kate at length accomplished her purpose.

" Now, I'll get along," she cried triumphantly, as a crimson drop oozed out and lay, slowly gathering volume, on the whiteness of her skin. "D . . ." Yes, that's all right now. ' Dear Mr. Gilmour; ' " and, as if there were no time to lose, Kate began to write a letter in which, in touching terms, she expressed her heartfelt gratitude, and characteristically entreated to be permitted to do " something more than hoist a handkerchief" towards effecting her escape from among the Masai. With a final injunction to Gilmour above all things to be careful of his life, Kate folded the note, and gave it to Ulu to carry to the tree, where the ingenious little damsel so bestowed it that that very night it was in the hands of its surprised and delighted recipient.

For the next three days Kate lived in a tremor of agitated expectation. Her chief anxiety was to form an accurate estimate of the number of warriors still remaining in the kraal, and to that purpose she kept Ulu incessantly on the watch for the arrival and departure of el-moran. Not content with second-hand information, she must needs, from time to time, brave all the annoyances attendant on her appearance abroad, and quit the hut to make observations for herself. The result was not encouraging. Though many warriors had already taken their departure, numbers still hung

about, recruiting on a course of milk after the
hardships of the late expedition. There would have
been even more, but, as Ulu had surmised, those
who were to form Kate's escort to Naivasha had
retired to the woods to eat flesh, according to their
custom when about to set forth on any trying
venture.

On the fourth day there were still a goodly
number of el-moran about, and Kate's heart sank
as she thought how much their presence would
increase the danger of any attempt at rescue that
Gilmour might risk.

At noon Ulu came in radiant, bearing the wazungu's "fetish messenger"—a note, which had
been left in the tree overnight.

"We have now everything in readiness," it ran,
"and only await your signal. If I do not ask you
to co-operate with me in the work we have before
us, it is simply because there is absolutely nothing
for you to do. I cannot enter into the details of
our scheme here; but, whatever happens, do not
leave your hut until I call you. In the midst of
the panic which we mean to raise send Ulu out
with the cry, 'Ngai has fled.' Keep up your hope
and your courage; I am most sanguine of success."

There was no chance of doing anything that
day; but when Kate made her appearance out of
doors next morning, to her intense delight she

found that all the warriors had left the kraal. She
waited until noon, lest a fresh relay should come
to take their place. Then, with a throbbing heart,
she watched Ulu, as she took a wet pocket-
handkerchief and spread it on the roof of the hut
as if to dry.

The sultry afternoon hours dragged wearily
along, and still no warriors appeared to crush
Kate's rising hopes. Impatiently she watched the
sun nearing the horizon. How slowly it seemed
to her to descend! In the cool of the evening
the cattle wended their way homewards to the
pleasant music of their tinkling iron bells, with
them a few herdsmen—cowards, and therefore
paupers—content to drag out an infamous existence
at the beck and call of their bolder brethren.

Among the cattle appeared Tanga, looking woe-
fully neglected and forlorn, his formerly well-
groomed coat now bedraggled and mangy. As she
remarked the donkey's subdued expression, Kate
felt a keen pang of regret at having recently paid
him so little attention, and at the thought that
now he must be left behind in the midst of such
uncongenial surroundings.

As he approached the spot where Kate stood,
Tanga recognized her at once, and, with brightened
eye and uplifted ear, trotted up to her, expectant
of the toothsome morsel which had usually been

his meed at Pisgah on similar occasions. But Kate had nothing for him—nothing but a dainty pat on the neck, a rub on the nose, and a sympathetic look into his meek, intelligent eyes. Tanga sniffed his mistress wonderingly when the accustomed biscuit was not forthcoming, a mute form of questioning which fairly went to Kate's heart.

With a final pat and a silent adieu, Kate turned away and re-entered her hut; while the herdsmen, unaccustomed to such passages, looked on silent and wondering. Had the two been talking to each other? Why should Ngai be interested in a donkey? were the mute questions that looked from every eye.

But Ngai's interest could not save Tanga from the common lot of his kind among the Masai, and, his mistress gone, he was driven, with cruel blows, back among the donkeys of baser breeds.

At length the sun sank behind the heights of Gelèi, and darkness rapidly settled over the face of the land. For a time there was a busy hum of voices, and the characteristic churr of cows being milked into calabashes. Then Ulu appeared, bearing the usual copious supply of milk, of which the greater part was set aside for use during the approaching flight.

The gate of the kraal was now carefully secured,

and, dreading no enemy, the inhabitants sought their huts, leaving only a number of boys to keep watch and ward, as much to inure the lads to warlike duties as from any imagined need.

Gradually the voices of men and women were hushed, and the impatient movements of the cattle, the occasional tinkle of a bell, the distant cry of beasts of prey, or the snarling of miserable pariah dogs alone betrayed the presence of life. The night was dark and overcast, and there was no moon. Through the intense blackness only the vaguest outline of the kraal was distinguishable.

In the pitch darkness of their hut Kate and Ulu sat awake and watchful, each silently clasping the other's hand. Every sound, every movement, fell upon senses strung to the highest pitch of excitement. Slowly the minutes crept on—minutes that seemed like hours. The suspense was fast becoming unbearable. Kate did not dare to think of all that was staked on this venture. If successful, it would give her back to life, her father, friends; if not, what other result could there be but destruction sure and certain to all concerned? Gilmour would be killed. He would die for her. No, no; not that. He would succeed. They would soon all be in safety. Backwards and forwards, so her thoughts swung, between sanguine hope and despairing apprehension. Was it to be life or was it to be death ? Life or death—life or death ? Oh, would the answer never come to that weary, terrible question ?

As if in response to her unspoken thoughts, there rang through the silent air the unmistakable crack of a rifle.

The supreme moment, then, had come !

CHAPTER XII.

Sharp, clear, and strong rose the warning voices of the boy watchers. In thundering reverberations the rocks and heights of Ndapdúk responded to the rifle-shot, and the echoes had not ceased before the men and women in the kraal had scrambled out of their huts and into the darkness of night.

In a hundred different tones they demanded an explanation. The boys, as much amazed as any, could give no intelligible answer. There was nothing but a confused babel of voices, darkness, and bewildering perplexity.

Again came the sudden flash from the murky gloom; again the unwonted sound thundered far and near. There was a terrified silence. Shivering with dread, each man stood staring into the surrounding blackness, unable to speak or move.

Ere they had time to recover, lurid tongues of flame shot upwards from the ground to the east, and there was a repetition of the awe-inspiring sounds, mingled with yet more deafening echoes. The west and the north followed suit, making confusion worse confounded.

The silence grew deathlike, with a dread too deep for words. As the crowd stood listening, mute and spellbound, to the reverberations once more dying away in the distance, the same questions hung trembling on every lip, "Was it Ngai who thus spoke? Were these the fierce scintillations of his eye in anger—these the dread terrors of his voice?"

Then from the darkness came a piercing cry, "Ngai has fled! Ngai has fled!" A shuddering gasp went through the horror-stricken crowd. Involuntarily they huddled closer together, to await whatever new terrors were in store for them.

As Ulu appeared in their midst, the women huddled around her, helplessly clutching her garments, and by speechless gesture imploring her protection. Unheeding the girl stood, wringing her hands in an apparent agony of grief and fear, and wildly repeating in anguished tones, "Ngai has fled! Ngai has fled!"

The paralyzed crowd was not left time to recover. Louder and nearer than before, the terrific noises burst forth anew. In the lightning flashes which accompanied them the figures of Gilmour's Zanzibaris were for a moment visible, appearing to the excited imagination of the beholders as frightful monsters—djins, servants of Ngai or Neiterkob (the spirit of evil). The terrified exclamations which rose to every lip remained unuttered. Clearly they were surrounded. What unknown and horrible fate was about to befall them?

Suddenly the thorn fence which enclosed the kraal was fired at three different points. Then madness seized the assembled multitude. The spell which held them mute was broken. Women and children wildly screamed to Ngai for help, and staid elders, losing all thought of self-possession, added their cries to the general clamour.

At length one man, of stronger will than the others, turned and fled towards the gate. Pell-mell, the rest rushed after him like sheep. The gate was closed, and in the crush it was impossible to open it or throw it down. But no power could now stop the panic-stricken mob. A few managed to shake themselves free, and, in their eagerness to escape, plunged madly into the fence, only to be torn by a thousand cruel spikes. The greater number, however, were driven against the gate with the united force of a hundred frantic human beings. Unable to bear the strain, the gate at last gave way, and out tumbled men, women, and children in a horrible, writhing, screaming mass, rolling over each other and treading one another down. With desperate struggles, the stronger scrambled to their feet again and continued their flight, heedless of the fallen comrades they left senseless on the ground.

With the roar and crackle of the burning thorns, the cattle also caught the panic. Bellowing with fear and madness, they stampeded, and dashed through hut and fence, knocking down men who ran, and trampling on others who lay prostrate.

Gilmour was now master of the kraal; but there was no time to be lost in taking advantage of his successful ruse. Unable longer to bear the suspense, Kate had quitted the hut the moment she saw the Masai in full flight. By the light of the fires, Gilmour could see her anxiously trying to pierce the outer gloom in search of her preservers; while Ulu, intoxicated with the excitement of the night, ran hither and thither like a limb of Satan.

"This way, Miss Kennedy," cried Gilmour, by way of apprising Kate of his whereabouts, at the same time springing right into the midst of the thorns, his legs safe in the protection of skin breeches.

Before Kate could reach him, he and Uledi had spread a couple of large skins over the huge acacia spikes of the fence, and scrambled to the inside of the kraal.

Kate gave a little gasp of relief as Gilmour

jumped down at her side. "Oh, Tom!" she began, unconsciously giving him the name by which it had pleased her to think of him ever since she had received his first letter; but the emotion of the moment was too strong for words, and a grateful pressure of the hand was the only conclusion of her sentence.

"Quick, Miss Kennedy! Jump into the skin," said Gilmour, lending her what help he could. "Don't be afraid; it's only Uledi," he added, as Kate started on noticing his hitherto unobserved companion. "Give him your hand. There! well done. Now, Ulu, over you go."

Gilmour followed, and next moment they were all safe outside the kraal. Not a minute too soon, however; for, the fence being like tinder, the fire was already close upon them.

Though out of the kraal, they were not yet out of danger. Their first consideration was to hurry beyond the circle illumined by the blazing huts and fence. A moment's halt was then called to see that all were safe, and at the same time pieces of skin were tied on over Kate's boots to prevent the formation of tell-tale heel-marks in the sand.

That done, as swiftly and silently as might be, the flight was continued. Behind, the kraal still burned up in a lurid circle of flame, shedding a bright light all around it for a considerable dis-

tance. From the surrounding darkness came
hundreds of excited voices, some eagerly questioning, others replying and spreading the dire intelligence of Ngai's fearful and wonderful flight. At
any moment the fugitives might be met by alarmed
Masai hurrying to learn the meaning of the fires
and of the strange noises, or by panic-stricken
stragglers flying for refuge towards the mountain.

Led by Uledi, the little band first pushed towards
the base of Ndapdúk, Kate deriving more encouragement than assistance from Gilmour's hand,
which all the while she held firmly clasped in her
own. Not a word was spoken, save when the guide
from time to time turned to those behind, to warn
them in a whisper of a bush, a hole, a stone, or
other obstacle that must be avoided.

In ten minutes they reached the mountain,
where they could breathe more freely, for there they
were out of the line of kraals and possible fugitives.
The clamour of voices sounded far and feeble, and
only a glowing ring of ashes told of the scene of
the recent fire. But for Gilmour and his followers
there could be no rest that night. An arduous
march to Dónyo Erók (black mountain) lay before
them, and it would go hard with them indeed if
they did not reach their destination before daybreak. By the aid of a match they consulted a
compass, and their course being set, they swiftly

pushed on again. A strict silence was still maintained, each one keeping eye and ear intently alert for any sign of approaching danger.

From time to time they were momentarily startled by the thunderous gallop of startled herds of zebra, or the noise caused by other game rushing recklessly through the bushes, disturbed by their approaching footsteps. To these common accompaniments of night marches in the wilds of Africa, Gilmour and his men were well accustomed, and only noted them to know them; but Kate, new to such experiences, got many a sudden fright, which her tightened clasp of Gilmour's hand was alone allowed to betoken.

With immense spirit, Miss Kennedy kept up the unwonted exertion of the trying march hour after hour. More than once Gilmour halted and urged her to rest, only to meet with persistent assurances that she was not in the least tired.

At last Kate was obliged to confess herself beaten, and a few minutes' halt was called. The tension somewhat relaxed, the men broke into congratulatory remarks. Kate alone was silent, held dumb by the very strength of her feelings. Gilmour, she knew by instinct, would readily understand her.

At this juncture Ulu's calabash of milk proved a veritable godsend, and did wonders in refreshing every one. But their halt must needs be of the briefest, for time was terribly precious. A great fear hung over them lest the mountain should not be reached before daybreak. Happily Kate's breakdown had been foreseen and provided for. Gilmour's hammock was turned out and rigged up on a pole carried for the purpose by one of the men.

At first Kate declared that she was quite able to walk again, but Gilmour would not hear of it. "In she must go," was his inexorable reply to all Kate's protestations that she did not require the hammock ; and in she did go, to be borne off almost at a trot, swinging between two stalwart Zanzibaris, and steadying herself by holding the pole.

The pale light of the waning moon now shed its mild effulgence over the plain, making walking more easy, and at the same time bringing out more clearly the dark outlines of Erok. From time to time the men who carried Kate changed shoulders, or stopped for a moment to allow others to take their place. Gilmour began to look nervously at his watch. There was no landmark to indicate how near they were to their goal. As seen it might be at any distance. Four o'clock came, and still they seemed to be getting no nearer it. In another hour it would be daylight. Resasi, one of Kate's bearers, stumbled once or twice and nearly fell. He was clearly played out. Gilmour ousted him from his place and shouldered the pole himself, with all the energy of a young athlete. As he trudged on in feverish excitement, unconsciously skinning his shoulder with the pole the while, he kept eagerly looking alternately towards the eastern horizon, and the hazy outlines of the mountain. But he could get no satisfaction, and kept panting on his way with contracted brow and clenched teeth, the veins of his neck and face strained almost to bursting by his unusual exertions.

It was now half-past four, and with an inward cry Gilmour remarked—or did he only imagine it?—the faintest possible streak of grey; and still the distance to be traversed was uncertain.

Uledi and Ferhani now took the pole, and, fresh from a rest, they trotted along with such vigour as almost to shake Kate out of the hammock. 4.40, and there was no mistaking the terrible fact that day was breaking, and all the men were exhausted.

"Stop!" cried Gilmour; "we'll have to run for it."

In silence Kate got out of the hammock, and scrambled to her feet. Gilmour took her hand. She was stiff and sore, and her feet were badly blistered; but as she warmed to her work the stiffness passed off, and all consciousness of pain was lost in excitement.

The imminence of the fugitives' danger was startlingly illustrated by their finding themselves running straight for a kraal. Another thirty yards and the inevitable clamour of scores of pariah dogs would have aroused the still sleeping inhabitants.

Unfortunately her first steady pace proved to be but a spurt on Kate's part. She felt her head begin to swim, and her legs to give way beneath her. She tottered rather than walked, and every moment it seemed as if she must sink down exhausted.

Gilmour remarked these symptoms with ever-rising apprehension. They were still in the open plain ; the mountain lay hid in mist and the day had broken. Discovery seemed certain. Their only hope lay in a raw fog, which providentially began to rise from the marshes of the Ngaré na Lala and obscured everything. Suddenly they found themselves between two kraals, which loomed through the surrounding greyness, portentously near. It was useless to turn back ; their way lay straight on, and, keeping a watchful eye on either hand, the little party pushed right ahead. At any moment a Masai might emerge from his hut, and then——

Kate stumbled, and, but for the supporting arms of Gilmour and Uledi, would have fallen.

"See, Bwana, see! There is smoke," half whispered Ferhani.

Gilmour turned his eyes towards the left-hand kraal. Sure enough, a column of smoke curled slowly upward and mingled with the overhanging mist.

"The game is up," he said to himself; "we shall be seen immediately.—Quick, some of you; bring the hammock again!" he added aloud, a baffled look on his face.

"Allah! some one moves!" gasped Resasi, his eyes fixed on the kraal to the right.

"Never mind me," cried Kate, letting go Gilmour's arm; "run, and save yourselves."

"Miss Kennedy!" exclaimed Gilmour indignantly.

"Look, Bwana, look!" eagerly interrupted Uledi; "we are close on the forest;" and he pointed to the shadowy outlines of the trees, now looming straight in front of them at no great distance.

"By Jove! so we are!" and, heedless of hammock or other assistance, Gilmour caught up the half-fainting girl in his arms. Gathering his exhausted forces together, with a powerful effort he ran rather than walked with her across the seventy or eighty yards of open ground that lay between

them and safety. Every moment he expected to
hear a Masai alarm sounding in his ears ; but
happily the mist veiled them in its protecting
wreaths. A minute or two of sustained effort, and
then, panting for breath and quivering in every
limb, Gilmour reached the sheltering confines of
the wood, where he sank down exhausted, and
deposited his precious burden on the ground.

For a moment Kate did not loosen her hold.
Slowly she unclosed her eyes, and lay looking at
her preserver in speechless gratitude. Then, unable otherwise to give expression to the feelings
with which her heart overflowed, she suddenly
drew his face down towards hers, and impulsively
kissed him.

CHAPTER XIII.

THAT kiss! What an unspeakable thrill it sent through Gilmour's being—new, strange, indefinable, incomprehensible. At first, as he lay upon the leaf-strewn ground, slowly recovering from the effect of his extraordinary exertions, he scarcely seemed to realize that there was anything unusual in Kate's impulsive embrace. He was too much overcome by exhaustion, his brain too benumbed from the severe strain he had recently undergone, to be capable of even the mildest wonder at any display of feeling, however unwonted. Gradually, however, as he became more alive to his surroundings, a sense of the full significance of what had happened began to steal upon him, and thrilled him with a vague delight. He did not in the least misunderstand the feeling which had prompted the sudden outburst on Kate's part, nor imagine that it arose from anything save the passionate desire to express an emotion otherwise inexpressible ; but it seemed worth all the anxiety and all the effort of the past two weeks to know that there was at least one soul on earth so genuine, so free, as to be able, in supreme moments, to rise above the common rationalism of custom and convention, and trust simply to the guidance of a pure and exalted feeling. He did not think of the dangers that might arise from general following of such a precedent ; he only thought that here beside him was a natural, true-souled woman, a woman with a heart, and——

Here a stolen glance at Kate revealed the fact that, however little he (Gilmour) might be inclined to blame or misapprehend her impulsive action, she herself had become distressingly aware of the possibility of his doing both. A painful flush overspread her cheeks and mounted to her temples as her eyes met his and were immediately averted.

The sight of Kate's embarrassment made Gilmour begin to feel embarrassed likewise. All of a sudden he seemed to become conscious that there was a palpable silence, and, much as he felt the necessity of breaking it, he could think of nothing coherent to say. Kate's fingers toyed nervously with the dead leaves on the ground beside her. Gilmour sat watching them with an interest as absorbed as if his life depended on the number they turned over in a given time. The silence grew more awkward every moment. Was nobody going to speak?

"Miss Kennedy," began Gilmour at length in desperation, commencing a sentence for the sake of saying something, and secretly trusting to Providence to finish it for him.

"Bwana," interrupted Uledi, opportunely, "we must be going further up the hill. We are not yet out of danger."

Kate looked up inquiringly.

Gilmour started. "You haven't seen any one coming our way, have you?" he asked.

"No, Bwana; but at any moment they *may* come. They are all astir now in the kraals down yonder;" and Uledi indicated the direction signified by a backward jerk of the head.

"By Jove! yes. And how the fog is lifting, too. They could almost see us if they knew where to look."

"Will the bibi have the hammock, Bwana?" asked Uledi, as he turned to rejoin the rest of the men. "Tubu says we can use it the first part of the way."

"Yes, certainly," began Gilmour.

"No, certainly not," interrupted Kate. "I can walk quite well now. It was the excitement as much as anything else that made me break down before. I'm sure I shall manage all right now the worst is over ; " and, in illustration of her renewed vigour, Kate clambered stiffly to her feet, and painfully limped a few paces.

" I'm afraid that won't do," began Gilmour.

" Yes, yes," insisted Kate ; "do let me try to walk. The stiffness will wear off as we go along."

"Take my arm, then," said Gilmour, yielding reluctantly. "See," he added, as he stooped to pick up a broken branch that was lying on the ground, "here is something that will do for a stick ; that ought to help you a bit ; " and only stopping to draw Kate's arm within his own, Gilmour called his little party together and prepared to ascend the mountain.

Tubu and Ferhani went first to act as guides, they, it will be remembered, having been before selected to seek out a hiding-place and prepare it for Miss Kennedy's reception. Always keeping within the confines of the forest, they held along the base of the mountain for a little, and then struck a game-path leading gradually upwards and eastwards. After a quarter of an hour's easy climbing, the ascent suddenly became more toilsome and difficult, and several times a halt was called to give Kate rest and breathing space.

"What a nuisance I am ! " she said, as, after one of these stoppages, she once more set her face determinedly upwards. "Just look at Ulu—how

she trots along. It would be almost worth while
to be a savage to possess such powers of physical
endurance."

Kate's remark was not without justice. Throughout all the breathless haste and agitation of that
exciting night the little M-Chaga had carried herself
with unflagging energy, showing a strength of wind
and limb not surpassed even by Gilmour himself.
She alone of all the little party seemed thoroughly
to enjoy the intense excitement of the more trying
episodes ; and now that it was nearly over, and
master and men alike felt the need of rest and
refreshment, she still appeared comparatively fresh
and lively.

Much of this arose, no doubt, from the implicit
confidence she had in Gilmour's power to bring
her safely out of every danger, and from the delight
she experienced in being once more beside her
beloved master. Beloved he certainly was by her,
in her own rude way, as was proved by her after
devotion to him in an hour of direst danger, and
under circumstances when all her savage instincts
would naturally have prompted her to think only
of her own safety.

Of the complex feelings he had awakened in
Ulu's darkened heart Gilmour suspected nothing.
In considering their respective relations one to
another, he had unconsciously laid more stress on

his feeling towards her than on Ulu's towards him. As he had so often said, he liked her as a man may his dog, she him as a dog may his master. Thinking only how little such a liking is to the man, who is capable of something so much better, he neglected to consider how much it may be to the dog, who is not capable of anything better. As Ulu patiently traversed the rocky pathway, Gilmour never dreamt of all the unspoken gladness that thrilled that "little soul" of hers in being near him, but in her buoyant step and elated expression saw only her natural, savage delight in any adventure that was stirring and unusual.

Truth to tell, he was not, that morning, thinking much of Ulu at all. More and more he became absorbed in looking after Kate, carefully piloting her across marshy places, picking her way for her where the ground was rough, and showing her a thousand other little attentions, expressive of an altogether new and more tender interest in her comfort and welfare.

At any other time Kate would almost have been inclined to resent such excessive solicitude on her behalf, her childhood's companionship with the boy-cousin with whom she had been brought up, and whose education she had shared, having early inspired her with a masculine dislike of being "mollycoddled." As it was, however, she was too utterly exhausted to take note with what anxiety Gilmour guarded her every step. Once or twice she acknowledged his timely assistance by a faint smile, or a murmured "Thank you," but for the most part she plunged doggedly on, intent only on the effort to keep her muscles in motion till her destination was reached.

At length, after about an hour's toilsome climb, Tubu and Ferhani abruptly left the narrow track, and entered a dense thicket. The rest of the party followed. Ten minutes' struggling through the bush and they suddenly emerged on a little woodland glade, which it scarcely needed Tubu's satisfied "Here we are, Bwana," to indicate was the haven of refuge they were bent on reaching.

A single glance sufficed to show Gilmour that, in entrusting to Tubu and Ferhani the task of seeking out and preparing a safe hiding-place, he had not made a mistake. The little glade was shut in on every side by a leafy screen of bush and creeper, one or two groups of graceful tree-ferns, which rose from its midst, greatly enhancing the charm of the scene.

The surrounding thicket was dense enough and remote enough to ensure security from discovery by adventurous herdsmen, the only people likely to find their way so far up the mountain. The interlacing branches of the trees and bushes formed a

pleasant shelter from the sun and wind, and a tiny
spring, that bubbled and sparkled temptingly in
the morning sunshine, promised constant abundance of clear, cool water.

On the day previous to the flight, all the goods
Gilmour had brought with him from Pepo-ni had
been removed from Ndapduk, and concealed at this
secluded spot. At the same time, Tubu and
Ferhani had run up two comfortable little huts,
one for Miss Kennedy and one for Gilmour, and,
in anticipation of a speedy return, had collected a
quantity of firewood, and laid it ready for lighting.

Bestowing a look of approval on his expectant
servants, Gilmour, with Kate still clinging to his
arm, at once made his way towards the larger of
the two huts and peeped in. It was empty, except
where in one corner lay a goodly heap of dry,
fragrant grass, to Kate's weary eyes looking the
sweetest, most desirable bed in the world.

"Oh, Mr. Gilmour, how good—how kind of
you!" she exclaimed gratefully, as Gilmour bade
her enter and take possession.

"Nonsense, Miss Kennedy; it's Tubu you have
to thank, not I. There now, sit down," Gilmour
added after a pause, in which he stooped down and
vigorously shook up the grass. "Wait a moment,
though; I must get you a rug first;" and, leaving
Kate to wonder vaguely in what way Mr. Gilmour's

extraordinary thoughtfulness would manifest itself next, he disappeared through the narrow doorway in search of the article desired.

When he came back, he found Kate kneeling on the ground, slowly unlacing her boots.

"You might have allowed me to do that for you," he said reproachfully, as he entered and noted the weary manner in which Kate raised herself from her stooping posture and, by the aid of his proffered hand, dragged herself to her feet.

"Oh no, Mr. Gilmour," she said, with a listless smile and a pathetic attempt to look lively; "you must really allow me to do *something* for myself. Oh, I am so tired," she added, as, with a sigh, she sank down on her grassy couch; "I can scarcely keep my eyes open."

"Then don't try to. Lie down and go to sleep at once," said Gilmour, cheerily. "Oh no, by-the-by, keep awake just a few minutes longer. Tubu is making you a cup of tea."

"Oh, I couldn't take it, thank you. I only want to sleep."

"Well, you can sleep after it comes. Meanwhile, I'll take myself off and leave you in peace;" and Gilmour quitted the hut, leaving Kate to wrap herself in her rug, and settle down snugly for the rest she stood so much in need of.

By the time he returned with the tea, Kate was

sound asleep and breathing quietly, oblivious of all troubles, mental and physical.

Noiselessly Gilmour turned away and betook himself to his own hut, first bidding Ulu find a place for herself in a corner of Kate's, and leaving his men to dispose of themselves as best they might under the shadow of the trees. Soon all were enjoying the most profound slumber, and silence reigned throughout the little glade, unbroken save by the constant trickle of the spring, the occasional note of a bird, or the heavy sigh of a sleeper as he turned in his sleep.

When Kate awoke, it was late in the afternoon. For some time she imagined herself to be still in her hut in the Masai kraal, and lay drowsily wondering what could be the meaning of the painful sensation of stiffness that pervaded her limbs. At length, she sat up and rubbed her eyes. They fell on the rug that covered her. Was she dreaming, or was she awake? She had no such rug as that in the kraal. She looked round. The hut was much larger than that to which she had been of late accustomed. From without came a soft murmur of voices, conversing in the pleasant, familiar Ki-Swahili dialect. Where was she? What had happened?

"Ulu, is the bibi awake yet?" called some one in accents that seemed familiar.

It was Mr. Gilmour. Yes, of course. She remembered everything now—the sudden firing of
guns, the blazing kraal, the panic-stricken Masai,
the rescue, the flight. In a few seconds Kate had
lived it all through again, and, shuddering, started
up to dispel the unpleasant vision.

As she cast her eyes around the hut, the first
thing they lighted on was a large calabash, standing on the ground ready filled with water, and
beside it (luxury of luxuries!) a cake of soap.
Hastily Kate undid her dress and flung it off.
Eagerly plunging her hands into the cool, refreshing water, she splashed it over her face and neck,
and rubbed the soap to a lather in childish delight.

Spite of its limited extent and the limited
dimensions of the basin, Kate thoroughly enjoyed
her wash, the first she had had for more than two
weeks that could truly be so called. Rather im-
perfectly, as may be supposed, she dried herself
with her handkerchief, and then cast a rueful look
at her sadly crushed and soiled white dress, the
original colour of which was now scarcely distinguishable after the smoke and dirt of the Masai
camp. With an expressive little grimace, which
plainly signified that its appearance was not at all
in keeping with her dainty ideas of personal neat-
ness, Kate held up the offending garment to the
light, and critically examined it.

"We must have a washing this very night," she muttered to herself, giving the dress a shake preparatory to putting it on.

She had just thrown it over her head, when she caught sight of something black protruding from under her rug, which, on rising, she had thrown in a heap to the foot of her lowly bed. On examination, the "something" proved to be a corner of the little canvas bag Kate had been taking with her to Pepo-ni on the day of her capture.

"Where on earth could he have got it?" she said to herself, rightly concluding that the bag had been placed there by Gilmour, but for the moment forgetting that she had ever brought it with her from Pisgah. As she opened it and discovered the dress and other odds and ends calculated so materially to add to her comfort, her eyes filled with grateful tears at this fresh proof of her preserver's kind considerateness.

"He's the best fellow in the world," she exclaimed, as she emptied the bag of its contents. "Dodo himself couldn't have been more kind and thoughtful."

It was only the work of a minute or two to brush out and coil the wavy masses of her luxuriant dark-brown hair, and don the welcome dress. Refreshed and smiling, she issued from the hut, all eagerness to greet Gilmour and tender him her heartfelt thanks.

CHAPTER XIV.

The little camp was now alive with preparation for the evening meal. A huge fire glowed cheerfully in the midst of the clearing, and round it squatted one or two of the men intent on superintending the roasting of some birds, which Uledi had succeeded in bringing down with his bow and arrow. Under one of the groups of the ferns, Tubu had already displayed his scanty stock of enamels, and a small kettle, which was "singing" inspiringly on another and smaller fire, reminded Kate of the tea Gilmour had promised to send her, and, now that she was sufficiently rested to be capable of thinking, excited her wonder as to where the tea was to come from.

"Good evening, Miss Kennedy," cried Gilmour, who, as soon as he saw Kate, jumped up from his seat under an mvulé tree, and advanced to meet her with outstretched hand. "I hope you have slept well?" he added anxiously, thinking that Kate still looked a little languid.

Kate took his proffered hand, and for a moment held it silently in both hers.

"Oh, Mr. Gilmour," she began at length, in a voice that trembled with emotion, "I wish you would let me thank you for all you have done for me—for the little things, such as this "—and Kate indicated by a downward glance the dress he had so thoughtfully provided—" as well as—— "

"Oh, but I won't," interrupted Gilmour hastily, his heart aglow with feeling, as he watched Kate's flushing cheek and swimming eyes, and felt as if he could willingly have sacrificed his life for this fair flower of womanhood, who all-unconsciously to both had gradually taken such a strong hold upon him, and who now, as utterly dependent on him, as possibly owing him her preservation from a fate worse than death, seemed in these last few hours to have grown inexpressibly dear to him. "There really isn't time, I assure you," he went on, laughing, delicately taking no notice of Kate's too evident agitation. "We are all starving of hunger, dinner is ready, and we only wait 'the sunshine of your presence' to fall to."

Kate bestowed on him a speaking glance, and smiled a little tearful smile, as he concluded his playful speech with a bow of mock courtesy, at the same time offering his arm to escort her to her seat, much as he might have done had they been chatting together in an English drawing-room before going downstairs to dinner.

No sooner was Kate comfortably established in the vicinity of the enamels, with her back against a tree, than Tubu appeared, carrying a well-filled plate for each of the two white people.

"Scarcity of dishes compels us to the splendour of a *diner à la Russe*, you see," said Gilmour, as he seated himself Turkish fashion, with his plate before him; "and scarcity of cutlery will necessitate my using my pocket-knife, if you don't mind," he continued, at the same time unclasping the article in question. "We did have two respectable table-knives once upon a time, but one has been lost *in transitu*, it seems."

"Don't apologize, Mr. Gilmour," cried Kate. "The marvel to me is not to find things missing, but to find them here. How did you contrive to bring everything? How could you so quickly arrange what to take and what to leave behind?"

"Oh, one soon comes to know what can be done without and what can't, when one is accustomed to camping out. Buffalo-hunting has been capital practice for damsel-hunting, I find."

Kate smiled. "But the idea of your bringing tea," she exclaimed, as Tubu at that moment handed her a fragrant cup of her favourite beverage. "I'm sure that's one of the things we might have done without. Aren't you going to have some yourself?" she asked in astonishment, as she observed that Gilmour was contenting himself with water from the spring.

"No; we keep our luxuries strictly for our guests."

"Oh, but I am not a guest; I'm a fellow refugee. You must have some."

"No, thank you."

"Yes," insisted Kate.

"But we can't afford it," objected Gilmour.

"Yes, we can. You shall have half of mine. There!" and before Gilmour had time to prevent her, Kate had emptied his cup of the water it contained, and half filled it with tea from her own.

"Well, I yield for once," said Gilmour, as he reluctantly took the cup Kate held towards him; "but, remember, it is the first and last time."

"We shall see," said Kate, a look of mischievous determination playing about the corners of her mouth. "*Skoll*," she cried, flourishing her tin cup as if it had been a golden goblet, and clinking it against Gilmour's ere she raised it to her lips, "I drink to the valiant Gilmour, and a happy issue to his gallant expedition."

"Amen," cried Gilmour, with a smile, glad to see Kate in such good spirits, and better pleased with this laughing tribute to his services than with a thousand more serious protestations of gratitude. There were depth and seriousness enough beneath all Kate's gaiety, he knew, and that was sufficient for him.

"What has come over Ulu?" queried Kate, suddenly pausing in her dissection of the rather tough piece of wild fowl which had fallen to her share.

"I sent her to my hut to make herself presentable, just before you came out. "I should fancy she would be here immediately."

"Oh, Mr. Gilmour, she has been such a comfort to me—more than a comfort, indeed, I should say. If it hadn't been for her I should have been killed. It was she who told the Masai that I was Ngai, and then showed me what to do to personate the character. She built a hut for me, and brought me food, and invented all sort of stories to keep me from being constantly tormented by my well-meaning but decidedly dirty and disagreeable worshippers. I was so dazed and helpless at first, I didn't seem to be able to think or do anything for myself, and Ulu thought and did for both of us. I don't know what I should have done without her."

"Then you like her?" asked Gilmour, his face lighting up with pleasure at Kate's unstinted praise of his whilom pupil.

"Like her? I love her!" cried Kate, emphatically. "I feel as if she were my sister. Ah, here
she comes!" she continued, suddenly interrupting
herself as Ulu at that moment appeared, looking
once more the graceful ideal of savage girlhood that
had excited Kate's admiration and astonishment,
as the child burst into Gilmour's sitting-room on
that sultry afternoon when Mr. Kennedy and his
daughter had first visited Pepo-ni.

"So my little mtoto has got a clean dress too,"
said Kate, affectionately putting her arm round
Ulu as she came running up, and gently pulling
her down beside her. "What a washing we shall
have, to be sure! I shall show you how to rub
the clothes as you saw them do at Pisgah. I think
the Bwana has seen me at a similar task before;"
and Kate looked smilingly towards Gilmour, to
find that he was forgetting to go on with his
dinner, and was intently gazing at her with eyes
full of admiration. "What is it, Mr. Gilmour?
Is anything wrong?" she asked hurriedly, mis-
reading the look, and casting a hasty glance over
her shoulder to discover the cause of her companion's inexplicable preoccupation. Those recent
days of constant dread and frequent alarms had
taught Kate to seek in the faces of those around
her forewarnings of danger rather than premonitions
of love.

"Oh, nothing—nothing," murmured Gilmour, confusedly, as he hurriedly began to ply his knife and fork. "I was only wondering what o'clock it is. I find my watch has stopped."

Kate looked at him in amazement, almost inclined to infer from his embarrassed manner that he *had* seen some cause of apprehension and did not wish to alarm her by telling her of it. She made no further remark on the subject, however, thinking that if there really was anything to fear she would know it soon enough.

"It is a quarter to seven," she said, looking at her watch, and professedly accepting the explanation Gilmour had chosen to give, though every moment she expected to see him rise on some pretext or other and give orders to his men to have their guns in readiness.

When he sat still and assiduously devoted himself to the consumption of his dinner, Kate felt reassured, and once more turned her attention to Ulu, whom, spite of Gilmour's remonstrances, she insisted on supplying with choice morsels from her own plate, while awaiting Tubu's arrival with one for the little maiden's self.

The meal finished, Kate settled herself comfortably for a long talk. Naturally enough, Gilmour was anxious to hear all she had thought, felt, and suffered during the days of her captivity; but not one word would Kate speak of herself until he had satisfied her regarding his own doings since the eventful day when the Masai war-cry had thrilled the woods of Pepo-ni with horror. In particular she insisted on a full account of all that had befallen her father up to the time Gilmour had parted with him. She had already heard from Uledi all that he could tell regarding the missionary's condition, and on the preceding night, before they had well left the Masai kraal, she had hurriedly assured herself, from Gilmour's own lips, that his wound was not dangerous, that there could be no doubt he would do well, and that, though of course distracted by the thought of his daughter's capture and its possible consequences, he had been able to pluck up faith and courage when Gilmour had spoken of starting in pursuit.

But now Kate must needs hear it all over again, down to the minutest detail of what her father had said and how he had looked. With professional interest she questioned Gilmour as to how he had dressed Mr. Kennedy's wound, and what orders he had left for his treatment, nodding approvingly every now and then as she listened to the patient recital.

" Poor papa ! " she exclaimed, when Gilmour had finished. " He will die of anxiety before we get back. If only we could have let him know we are at least so far out of danger ! "

"I'm afraid that is impossible," said Gilmour, gravely.

"Oh yes, I know." "There's nothing for it but to wait. How long do you think we shall have to stay here?"

"Until the Masai have somewhat got over the excitement of your flight, I suppose. I should say not less than a fortnight, at any rate."

"A fortnight?" repeated Kate, in a distressed tone. "Oh, Mr. Gilmour, what *will* poor papa do? Couldn't we set out soon, and travel during the night?"

Gilmour shook his head. "I'm afraid not. You couldn't cross the plain in one night, and we should certainly be discovered if we attempted it during the day at present. Then you couldn't stand the fatigue yet. I don't believe the men could either, after all they have just come through," he added hastily and perhaps not quite truthfully, as he noticed Kate's disappointed look. "Be sure we shall start as soon as it is at all safe."

With this assurance Kate was obliged to be content. There was no use rebelling against Fate, and Fate for the present seemed to have decreed she was not to see her father for some time to come. Meanwhile another hour was pleasantly spent in hearing the particulars of Gilmour's journey in pursuit, and relating her own experiences among the Masai. Then Kate made Gilmour show her his little commissariat, the discovery of each new article provided for her comfort eliciting on Kate's part fresh exclamations of wonder and delight at her companion's extraordinary kindness and forethought.

"Oh, Mr. Gilmour," she exclaimed warmly, when a little later she said " Good night," " I should be quite happy now if it weren't for the thought of papa ! If only I could know he wasn't worrying too much ! " and Kate sighed heavily as she entered her hut, where Ulu lay already buried in slumber, and where she herself, spite of the trouble at her heart, soon likewise lay sleeping soundly.

Tired as he was, it was long ere Gilmour fell asleep that night. His anxieties forgotten, he lay in a vague, happy dream, his mind filled with but one image—the image of the woman to whom he had that day given life and liberty. Her face was yet before his eyes, her voice yet sounded in his ears, her touch yet lay warm upon his hand. He thought no more of this or that word she had spoken, this or that deed she had done. It was *herself*—all she was and all she might be, whether that were good or evil—that possessed his soul, and filled it with a dear, dim, sweet, unreasoning delight. Ah, Tom Gilmour, what of thy dear-bought wit, thine old experience of woman's fickle-

ness, thy vows of eternal celibacy now? Forgotten
—all forgotten. My young friend Tom, it is all
over with you—you are swiftly, surely, sadly,
madly, falling head over ears in love.

CHAPTER XV.

A FORTNIGHT passed by with surprising swiftness. It was wonderful how quickly time sped in that retired little nook on the lonely mountain side; how happily, too, spite of the ever-present problem which Kate and Gilmour discussed with each other every day : How were they to get away from Dónyo Erók, and reach Pepo-ni in safety?

It must be confessed that this question pressed much more heavily on Gilmour than on his fair companion. Like Ulu, Kate placed implicit confidence in Gilmour's power to bring her safely through whatever difficulties might be in store for them. Moreover, Miss Kennedy was naturally of a buoyant and hopeful temperament, and, though she clearly understood the nature of the dangers they had mostly to fear, it seemed impossible for her to look on them as more than incidental—as obstacles merely, which might be altogether evaded, and at the worst could but be met and overcome.

The thought that she might never reach Pepo-ni

at all was one which Kate never allowed herself to
entertain for a moment. Her one real anxiety was
for her father. Try as she would to believe Gilmour's comforting assurance that Mr. Kennedy
would be " all right," as was Gilmour's broad way
of putting it—that he was prepared not to expect
their return for some weeks, and, from the fact that
he heard no news of the fate of the little rescue
party, would conclude that the news, if he could
hear it, was good, Kate could not rid herself of the
idea that her father's anxiety on her behalf might
seriously retard, if not altogether hinder, his re-
covery from his wound. Her only consolation lay
in the hope that, as Mr. Kennedy would be sure to
keep the neighbourhood constantly on the alert for
any news of their movements, he might at last
catch some vague rumour of " the flight of Ngai,"
and would construe it as meaning that his daughter
had made her escape from the hands of the Masai,
and was at least so far safe.

Though not quite so sanguine on this point as
Kate, Gilmour took good care to keep it constantly
before her mind, firmly believing in the Shake-
spearean adage of the merry heart, and bent on
keeping Kate bright and cheerful whatever evils
might betide.

Thus constantly thrown together as our two
young friends were, they came to know and under-

stand each other better in a few days than they would under ordinary circumstances in as many years. They had everything and did everything in common, and, finding each other more and more congenial, their mutual liking flourished and grew apace. Happy in each other's society, time never hung heavy on their hands, though apparently life at the Anchorage, as Kate had christened their secluded retreat, presented but little variety. An extra good "bag" made by Tubu or Ferhani, the recital of Uledi's frequent reconnoitring expeditions, a daily climb to some coign of vantage whence the plain beneath could be closely scanned by the aid of a glass—these were the only excitements which varied the monotony of the long, quiet days.

But, then, that monotony—to two people who, like Kate and Gilmour, were not dependent on externals for happiness, how pleasant it was! Meals not always plentiful, but eaten with good appetite and good temper; long rambles together through the depths of the forest; long talks in the starlight or in shady nooks under the trees when the afternoon sun made greater exertion impossible. Of what they talked, what pen shall describe? Much of their situation, no doubt, and much of other things in no way connected with it; much also of themselves, as youthful lovers ever will, in their eager anxiety to make themselves understood.

Lovers! Ah, that was just what Gilmour would
have liked to know if they dared call themselves.
It had not taken him many days to discover in
what light he had come to regard the true-souled,
warm-hearted girl beside him, whose gratitude and
confidence found mute expression in her every look
and gesture, but whose deeper feelings towards
him he could not surmise.

Much as he would have wished to believe it,
Gilmour could not think Kate was in love. The
easy, friendly manner in which she treated him,
her perfect frankness and openness, were too unlike
the shyness and silence that mark the dawn of a
deeper passion than mere friendship. And yet
who could tell? One word from him, the faintest
whisper of his own daily deepening love, and might
not her sisterly liking change to love likewise?
Yes; but if it were not so, if Kate did not recipro-
cate his affection, what then? To speak would
only be to bring their present happy, unembarrassed
intercourse to a close. Besides, was he not in
honour bound to wait until Kate was once more
back under the guardianship of her father, lest he
should seem to take undue advantage of her grateful feelings, and of her dependence upon him in
their then position?

Then what if Kate already loved another? What
of this cousin of hers, this Dodo, about whom Gil-

mour intuitively felt there was some mystery which
Kate had never explained to him? He was the
only one of all her friends about whom she never
would talk freely, the one whose name soonest of
all made her grow sad and silent, and brought to
her eyes the wistful look Gilmour had learned to
connect with her passionate attachment to her
girlhood's home, and her longing for the life of
which it had been to her the centre. In these
days of constant companionship, Gilmour had come
to know what that life had been, down to its
minutest details. He had made the acquaintance
of every one of Kate's student friends, and knew
all the little idiosyncrasies of the various members
of her uncle's household—all but those of Dodo,
about whom Kate never got farther than that they
had been "just like brother and sister." It was
very unsatisfactory, very puzzling, Gilmour felt;
and yet what right had he to seek to know more?
He had always been extremely reticent in speaking
to Kate of his own former life; why should he
expect her to be more communicative in regard to
hers? Perhaps some day he *would* tell her all
there was to tell about himself, and how it was he
had come to be the pessimistic, dissatisfied individual she had first known; and then perhaps he
would learn about her the one thing he most
wanted to know, which was also apparently the

one thing about which she at present chose to be silent. Sooner than he expected, it came about that Gilmour did both.

Though for the most part reserving his doubts and perplexities for the privacy of his hut, and in Kate's society giving himself up to the immediate pleasure of being near her, he could not always hide his trouble and smother care in smiles. There were times when the desire to speak to her and tell her of his love almost overmastered him, and he would sit speechless beside her, not daring to open his lips lest the forbidden words should pass.

Kate was not slow to note these frequent silent moods, and the careworn expression which accompanied them; but she attributed them solely to his anxiety regarding the manner of their final deliverance, and made a point of rallying him out of his dejection, while expressing her cheerful confidence in his ability to effect their safe escape.

They were sitting together at breakfast one morning. Gilmour had had a bad night; he looked weary and down-hearted. Kate was all sympathy and kindness.

"Tom," she began—they had long ago dropped the formal Miss and Mr.—"you really let things worry you far too much. I shall think you are sick of me, if you look so gloomy because you don't see your way to getting rid of me at once."

Getting rid of her! Poor fellow! Gilmour felt at that moment as if all he wanted to make him happy was to know that he might keep her by him for ever. Kate's laughing words sounded cruel.

"Tom, *will* you wake up?" she went on, bending towards him, and tugging at his sleeve with pretended impatience, as he sat gazing at her in silence with absent eyes. "I never saw you so persistently dismal before. What is the matter?"

"I am growing old," answered Gilmour, with a little, wintry smile that somehow made him look very old indeed.

"'A subjective fact of universal experience,' Tom! Don't let that trouble you. Like the way to the altar, 'It's the road we've a' tae gang.'"

Gilmour smiled again, this time a little more cheerfully. "To-day I pass a milestone then," he said. "It's my birthday."

"Your birthday, Tom! Why didn't you tell me?" cried Kate, reproachfully. "May you live a thousand years," she went on, shaking hands with him by way of congratulation.

"I don't want to, if the next nine hundred and seventy are to be no better than the last thirty," was Gilmour's gloomy reply.

"Bear!" ejaculated Kate, with a smile and a look that made the uncomplimentary epithet seem almost like a term of endearment. "Whatever your grudge against the world is, forget it for to-day. We must celebrate your birthday. To begin, you shall have one of my sardines."

"No, I shan't," asserted Gilmour, decidedly.

"Yes, you shall—you must," said Kate, with equal decision. "Just this once," she continued in a more coaxing tone; "this is a special day, you know."

"You are always discovering 'special' days," grumbled Gilmour. "This is the third this week. To-morrow you will want me to have something else, because it's Friday, and not Thursday, and is therefore a 'special' day."

Kate laughed. "No; my generosity comes to an end now—like the sardines;" and, with an air of profound satisfaction, Kate fished the last succulent teleostean from its bath of oil, and laid it on Gilmour's plate.

She had always considered it a grievance that Gilmour would not share with her the luxuries he had been at the trouble of bringing from Pepo-ni, and she hailed with delight each visible decrease of the little store, as approximating the time when she must be permitted to rough it with the rest. Gilmour, on the other hand, viewed the daily diminution of his supplies with ever-rising apprehension, which on this occasion served materially —he alone knew how materially—to lessen his enjoyment of the delicacy Kate, in her ardent desire to *fête* him, had so wilfully insisted on his accepting.

Loving her as he did, and anxious as he was to save her from hardship, Gilmour could not share Kate's cheerful indifference in looking forward to the near possibility of discomfort and privation. On this morning in particular he seemed unable to enter into Kate's good spirits, her lively sallies only serving to deepen the downcast mood in which he had awakened. As the meal proceeded, he grew more and more laconic in his replies, and finally relapsed into absolute silence. For a time Kate left him to his own thoughts, and sat quietly beside him, watching his troubled face with anxious eyes.

"Still nursing that grudge, Tom," she said at length, purposely ignoring nearer sources of possible disquietude, and looking up into his face with a sympathetic smile. "Won't you tell me what it is? Perhaps it wouldn't look so grievous then."

Gilmour started. For a moment he did not understand to what Kate alluded. He had not been thinking of himself, but of her and of all that lay between him and the time when he had made up his mind he might venture to speak freely of his feelings towards her. Then he recollected.

"Tell you my grudge against society, you mean. I haven't got any—not now, at least."

" No ? Tell me what it *was*, then."

" That would be a long story, I'm afraid. I should have to go over my whole life."

" Well, why not ? Time is no object with us here ; " and Kate settled herself comfortably in her favourite attitude for listening.

Why not, indeed ? thought Gilmour, as he sat for a moment with earnest eyes fixed on Kate's expectant face. There was nothing in the record that he need be ashamed of, except, indeed, his too hasty flight to Kilimanjaro, and of that Kate already knew, and liked him notwithstanding. She might like him even better perhaps if she knew of what terrible disappointment that flight had been the outcome, and how his early environment had fostered the feelings which caused him to take his disappointment more bitterly to heart than would most men who knew the world as he knew it.

All his life Tom Gilmour had been a dreamer and an enthusiast. Born in a peaceful valley among the southland Scottish hills, his boyhood had been spent among conditions tending most effectually to foster his naturally poetic and romantic bent.

The scene with which the uncomprehending eyes of his childhood had gradually become familiar was one of unequalled loveliness. Probably throughout the length and breadth of Britain there is no other spot so perfect in itself, so complete in every natural charm, as that broad, lowland valley, which Gilmour now described with a graphic minuteness which spoke eloquently of his love for its every well-known detail.

Far surpassed in any one feature by a score of places, in its varied assemblage of pleasing characteristics, the scenery of Carrondale stands alone. Stretching away from the little village in their midst, the fertile fields spread their rich mosaic of gold and green around cosy farmhouses breathing of peace and plenty. There the broad home-park, with its stately array of oak and beech and broad-leaved chestnut, gives added dignity to lordly mansions, stern with the pride of high degree. Beyond, the well-clad ridges lose themselves in purple heath or desolate moorland, or rise into swelling hills, over whose towering shoulders the fleecy clouds linger in loving dalliance, to cast a mantle of magic shadow athwart their hoary sides. Below, in broken reaches, gleams the river, loitering seawards between wooded banks or smiling corn-fields. Its tributary streams, in haste to join it, rush headlong over riven rock, and linn, making glad music in many a dim retreat, the sacred haunt of poetry and love.

Every glen, almost every field, has its story of

the romantic, half-forgotten past. Yonder is the still faintly traceable camp of the Pict; further off rises his grass-grown burial-mound. Many a hill-top tells where Roman legions halted; the road which they traversed still shows green against the darkness of its heath-clad slopes. In such a linn, the inhabitants love to tell you, the Covenanter sought refuge from "bloody persecutors;" on such a bleak ridge was he shot dead. Here a monument by the wayside tells where a martyr fell; there a simple tablet marks his grave in some nettle-grown kirkyard. Many an ivied ruin, stronghold of the warrior lords and chartered robbers of ruder days, speaks eloquently its own dread tale of cruel encounter, stern resistance, siege, surrender, and death.

What more could Nature afford or history supply to fire the fancy and rouse the romantic instincts of a lad naturally prone to poetic imaginings? Eagerly Gilmour drank in every tale of knightly chivalry in love and war, every legend that appealed to the imagination by its terror or its pathos, supplying the gaps in the record by much erratic reading of poetry and prose, better fitted for the education of a Don Quixote than for the training of the more practical knight of the nineteenth century.

As the years passed by, however, he began to

think less and less of the romantic aspect of his surroundings, and more and more of the wonderful lesson they had to teach of Nature and Nature's ways of working. In his attempts to decipher the rock-told story, he was led into every secluded corner of the valley, every wild nook of the hills and moorlands. Nature became his religion. In a sense, he was a Pantheist, worshipping everything, from the storms to the sun and the hidden soul which unites them.

Happiest when alone, he would climb to some distant height, to revel in the glorious freedom of the fresh mountain air, or gaze in ecstasy on all the varied loveliness of the valley at his feet. Or he would spend the long, slow hours of summer noon lying among the heather, his senses lulled to dreaminess by the far-off bleat of sheep, the whirr of grouse, the mournful call of the curlew, as they blended harmoniously with the restful sound of unseen burn, or the distant sough of brawling torrent.

What longings and aspirations filled his soul the while! Vague and crude enough, no doubt; but all upward, all towards the light. His heart was all in the future, all in the coming battle of life, all in the strife against falsehood and wrong-doing, and on the side of truth and right.

Such friends as he had were no less imaginative, no less enthusiastic than himself. He was one of a little coterie of boys, no two of them with the same ambition in life perhaps, but all with the same ideals, the same aspirations. Vowing eternal brotherhood, each in due time set out to pursue the course he had marked out for himself, Gilmour at length betaking himself to the university, in pursuit of the scientific studies to which he was devoted. In the midst of the city's thronging thousands he was even more alone than among his native hills. Reserved and happy in his own thoughts, he did not court society, and, as he made no special claim to distinction, society did not court him. One or two of his former schoolfellows still kept up the old, familiar intercourse, but new friendships he neither made nor desired.

At the end of four years, Gilmour, his university career completed, returned to his father's house the same dreamy enthusiast he had quitted it, his idealism intensified, his faith in man unshaken, his theories of life as loftily impracticable as they well could be.

The time had now come, however, when he must do, not dream. Important business, undertaken on behalf of his father, called him to the East. His lot was cast in an out-of-the-way part of China, where he had but little society. Such as he did have consisted chiefly of men of the world, worshippers of money and of pleasure mostly, with

none of his own high-flown notions regarding right
and wrong, virtue and vice, good and evil. As far
as he could, he held himself aloof, choosing to
regard his ill-assorted, but unavoidable, companions
as exceptions to the usual rule of human conduct
(which, indeed, to some extent they were), rather
than lower by a hair's breadth his own exaggerated
idea of what he conceived that rule to be.

After two years, Gilmour revisited England.
During his absence he had had but little communication with his friends; but he thought of
them daily, and continually looked forward to the
pleasure of meeting them again. The meeting
came, and with it the first real chill in his life.
The greeting of former companions lacked its expected cordiality. Gilmour seemed to have become
indifferent or but as other people to those who had
been wont to receive him with more than brotherly
warmth. Many of them, too, seemed to have fallen
away from the high ideals they had formerly held
in common, and, almost without exception, in
making their first great step in life, they had
altered the standpoint from which they viewed
men and the world.

It was a bitter disappointment. Gilmour was
unconscious that he, too, had altered and ripened,
and he made no allowance for the fact that, while
he had practically lived in isolation, and thus had

perhaps exaggerated the value of the former bonds, his friends had continued amongst congenial society, and formed new friendships to atone for the interruption of the old.

Chilled and saddened, Gilmour hailed with relief the time when he must once more go abroad. Fortune now led him more into the highways of life. In the rough push and jostle of the crowded thoroughfare there was no more time for dreaming. Gradually it dawned upon him that the real world was not the world he had imagined, nor men the high-souled, high-principled beings he had fondly believed. Everywhere there seemed to be a compromise between justice and truth, and what were called the necessities of business, politics, and society. Everywhere the tendency seemed to be to sacrifice duty to self-interest, what was right to what would "pay" financially or socially. Disinterestedness was a motive unknown to all, incredible by any. Money, position, and pleasure were the goals of universal ambition and universal effort.

Before the enormity of the evil with which he everywhere found himself confronted, Gilmour at first stood stupefied. He felt helpless, and his helplessness made him apathetic. At times he feebly struggled, but, overwhelmed by the character of his awakening, he could throw no enthusiasm into his resistance. A dreadful feeling came over him that he, too, would in time succumb to the influence of his surroundings, and sink to their low beastly level, till he could contemplate sin with an easy smile or an indifferent shrug of the shoulders, and devote himself heart and soul to the world's hideous fetish, "Getting on."

Inevitably, like so many others, he would have done so, had it not been for one dream he still cherished, one influence which still held sway over him, and, more than any other, served to hold together the remnant of his faith in human nature.

That influence was one Gilmour could not well trust himself to speak of even now—even to the woman through whom, unconsciously, faith and hope had once more been revived within him, spite of the final dissipation of his last illusion. The memory of that bitter disappointment still had power to agitate him. He hesitated and paused in his hitherto fluent recital, to which his companion had listened almost in silence, content to show her sympathy and interest by look rather than word. Half guessing what was coming, for some moments Kate still sat silent; then, with eyes full of mingled pity and tenderness, she leant forward, and gently laid her hand on Gilmour's.

"Never mind now, Tom," she said softly. "I think I can understand. You will tell me the rest some other day."

CHAPTER XVI.

KATE's kindly words and gesture touched Gilmour deeply. For a moment he forgot himself, his past, his resolution to be silent—everything but his love for Kate and his longing to tell her of it. But the power of speech seemed to have forsaken him. He seized the hand she had laid on his and fervently kissed it. Kate drew back in alarm, too much astonished even to feel indignant.

"Mr. Gilmour—Tom! What is it?" she began.

Her altered tone recalled Gilmour to his senses. "Forgive me, Kate," he stammered; "I am not myself this morning. Come," he continued more calmly, as he pulled himself together with a determined effort, conscious of Kate's wondering eyes still fixed on him inquiringly, "let me tell you the rest of my story;" and, leaving Kate no time for further conjecture, Gilmour plunged hastily into the history of his ill-starred first love.

On the eve of his departure for the East the first

time, Gilmour had one evening been casually
introduced at the house of a friend to a Miss Nina
Lindsay, the daughter of an Edinburgh advocate.
The lady was young, scarcely seventeen, and gave
promise of being very beautiful. Gilmour conversed with her a good deal, and felt greatly taken
by her simple, ingenuous manner and sprightly
talk. Going abroad, however, almost immediately,
he had no opportunity of seeing her again, and
had indeed almost forgotten her, when, on his
return to Scotland, they again met, this time at a
dance, where Nina was the observed of all observers.
She had grown very lovely—perfect almost in form
and feature, it seemed to Gilmour, who was not
long in reminding her of their former slight
acquaintance. She looked pleased to see him
again, and danced with him several times that
evening, to the undisguised chagrin of other
would-be partners, who considered their claim to
favour superior to that of the stalwart, sun-browned
traveller.

After that Gilmour and Miss Lindsay saw a
great deal of each other. He paid her marked
and devoted attentions, and she, on her part,
seemed nothing loth to receive them. Still, he
said nothing to her of love, fearing the results of a
premature declaration, and conscious that, even
supposing she loved him in return, it would yet in

all probability be some years before he could offer her a home such as he conceived would be becoming this bright, beautiful, dainty creature. When he returned to the East, it was with a new object in life. It was not for himself, not for his father even, that he worked, but for Nina—Nina, who was good as she was fair, noble and high-souled as she was vivacious and fascinating; Nina, his love, whom one day he hoped to make his wife.

Suddenly his father died, and, sooner than he expected, Gilmour found himself master of a considerable fortune. He returned to Scotland and hastened to Edinburgh. Nina was married—had been married a year—married, too, to some bantling millionaire whom she made no pretence of loving, and who openly boasted that he had bought her for the diamonds with which he strewed her wedding-gown.

"I could have forgiven her," Gilmour went on bitterly to Kate, "if she had not seemed happy in her degradation. It was that which made me mad, and shattered the last fragment of my faith in human nature."

Kate looked intensely sympathetic. "You saw her again, then?" she asked gently.

"Yes, once, at a ball. She looked perfectly radiant. 'Glad to see you back again, Mr. Gilmour,' she said lightly, as she passed me by, hanging on her husband's arm. ' Come and see us soon. My day is Wednesday.' After that I don't know what would have happened. I should have gone headlong to perdition, I suppose, had it not been for a lucky chance. One day I was idly turning over the leaves of a recent work on exploration in Central Africa, when the idea to go there suddenly flashed across my mind. The life seemed to promise excitement, perhaps forgetfulness. I made the necessary preparations and went. I came to Kilimanjaro and settled down there. The rest you know."

Yes, Kate knew. Already Gilmour had told her how, in the loneliness of Pepo-ni, his soul had craved for some one to care for, and how he had hoped to find in Ulu some satisfaction for that craving. How his failure had anew aroused the desire for fellowship with his kind, and how that desire had been stimulated by his meeting with herself. How he had finally resolved to return to Europe, and had but awaited her visit to Pepo-ni to apprise her of his intention, when the fulfilment of it had to be postponed on account of her capture by the Masai. Kate knew it all, but at that moment she did not care to recall it. Her mind was busy over Gilmour's love trouble, the narration of which had revived the memory of her own; for Kate, Beatrice-like as her attitude towards men had ever been, and little as she had thought of love and marriage, was too winning and winsome not to have had many admirers—lovers even, chief among whom had been her cousin Dodo. Upon Dodo, who had been the constant companion of her childhood and girlhood, Kate had ever looked as on a brother. But to him Kate was more than sister, and it was partly the discovery of this that caused her to consent with unexpected readiness to her father's request that she should quit Europe and postpone the completion of her medical studies till some future time.

It was strange, Kate thought, how love should have brought both Gilmour and herself to Kilimanjaro—he because he could not get, she because she could not give, the satisfaction love desired. More keenly than ever before she seemed to realize how much her refusal must have meant to Dodo—how terrible might have been its results!

"It was different with him, though," she said, unconsciously thinking aloud. "At least, he cannot have been disappointed in *me*. I have done nothing unworthy of myself. Ah, Tom," she went on sadly, becoming suddenly aware of Gilmour's inquiring look, "I have had love troubles too. It was Dodo," she continued hesitatingly, her eyes averted, her colour rising, as if she doubted her right to reveal Dodo's secret. "He loved me—he wanted me to be his wife; but I couldn't, you know—I couldn't;" and in her agitation a tear trickled slowly down Kate's cheek and fell on Gilmour's hand.

Gilmour started as if it had burned him. "Kate, Kate," he burst out passionately, "I too love you—I too——" Then he stopped, struck dumb by the frightened expression in Kate's tell-tale eyes.

"Hush, Tom, hush! don't say it," she gasped, clasping her hands in an agony of entreaty.

"Oh, Kate, tell me——"

"No, no, no! Don't ask me. I can't—I can't. Oh, Tom!" Kate broke off suddenly, and, burying her face in her hands, she burst into a wild fit of sobbing, all the more painful that she tried hard to suppress it.

Before this vehement outbreak Gilmour sat help-less, with drawn lips and cheeks white from the effort to command himself. He tried to speak; but before he could say a word to comfort her, Kate darted to her feet, and sought refuge in her hut.

With a despairing groan, Gilmour turned over on the ground, and hid his face in his arms. It was out, then—the secret which had been trembling on his lips for a week and more was out, spite of his determination that Kate should not know it until relieved of what she might consider the indebtedness of her present position. It was out, and with its revelation his hope had vanished, his doubts had come to an end. As yet the agony of disappointment seemed dull and dead; the termination to his uncertainty was almost a relief. "She does not love me; she does not love me," he repeated to himself again and again, as if by constant iteration his brain must at last realize the full import of the words, and awake to the anguish of their meaning. But no; he could only lie there on the grass, stunned and stupefied, a strange, aching numbness at his heart, as if it were wrung well-nigh to breaking.

By-and-by he roused himself. What was Kate doing? Crying her heart out for grief at the pain she had caused him? He must go to her, and try to soothe and comfort her; bid her forget what he had said, and sue for the right to continue as her brother, since he might be nothing more. He rose and walked slowly towards the hut. As he approached, he heard a low sound of weeping, and caught a glimpse of Kate, seated in a corner, with Ulu on the ground beside her.

"Bibi, speak to me," said the little girl, pulling at Miss Kennedy's gown. "Was the Bwana angry with you?"

The only answer was a stifled sob.

"I will go to the Bwana and tell him you are sorry," said Ulu again, half rising and looking wistfully at Kate, at a loss how to construe her violent emotion. "He will not be angry any more."

"No, no, mtoto. He is not angry. Don't go away; you must stay beside me;" and Kate threw her arms around her humble consoler, and clung to her, crying more quietly, as if she derived some hidden comfort from the human contact.

Gilmour did not stay to see more. They seemed to understand each other, the two women, great as was the gulf which separated them, and he felt as if it were better to leave them to themselves. Hastily turning away, he plunged into the wood. For long he wandered on and on, sometimes sauntering along in gloomy dejection, sometimes crashing wildly through crackling bush and breaking branch, seeking an outlet for the stormy unrest of his soul in fierce physical exertion. He did not return to camp until late in the afternoon. As he drew near, he could see Kate sitting with Ulu under the tree-ferns.

Kate's face wore a quiet, subdued look; her eyes bore evident traces of recent tears. She had fought a hard battle with herself that day. In the shock of Gilmour's sudden and unlooked-for confession, it had not at first occurred to her to think how

much or how little he was to her. He was a friend
merely, whom as a friend she dearly loved, and it
grieved her beyond measure to know him grieved.
There must be something fatal about her, she said
to herself. This was the second time now that
she had had to inflict a cruel wound on one who
had been to her as more than brother. "More
than brother!" Kate started at the thought.
Yes, she did like Gilmour more than a brother,
more than Dodo even, than whom she had believed
she could never hold any one dearer on earth.
Was it because she owed him her liberty, perhaps
her life? Was it because he was her protector,
her only companion? No; she felt sure it was
none of these. She liked him for himself, without
why or wherefore. But, then, that liking—it was
not love. Ah no; for love ended in marriage, and
Kate did not want to marry. She felt quite, *quite*
sure of that. The very idea of it was distasteful to
her. Give up her freedom, her dreams of an
independent future, her schemes for wide, active
work in the world, and cramp herself to the narrow
sphere of a household and the dismal routine of
domestic duties? No, no, no; Kate certainly was
not in love. She could not make so great a
sacrifice, even for Tom Gilmour. And yet how
much he had done for her; how much he had
risked; how good, how kind he had been; and she

—how very, very ungrateful she must seem to him. Well, she could not marry him out of gratitude ; it would be unjust to Tom, as well as to herself. Besides, it was not gratitude Tom wanted, but love, and love she did not, could not, so long as love implied marriage with all its fearful possibilities. "I only wish I *could* fall in love," she had sobbed out ; "perhaps marriage wouldn't seem such a horrible bugbear then."

Of course it wouldn't, little woman ; and by the time you are a little older, perhaps you will discover that independence does not necessarily imply living alone in the world, and that our efforts to do good are not rendered less effectual by the fact that we share them with another. Love binds our hands ; but it binds them not to fetter, but to stay.

As yet Kate did not know that, however, and in her little hut on Dónyo Erók there was no one to comfort her with the words of wisdom and experience ; so she must needs sit sad and tearful through the long hours of that summer afternoon, inwardly sentencing herself and her lover to many days of needless misery, all because she could not read her woman's heart aright, through the mist of warped ideas and grievous misconceptions that filled her foolish little head.

As Gilmour approached the place where she sat, Kate felt the tears start to her eyes again ; but she resolutely choked them back, and managed to speak to him, if not without a mental quiver, at least with outward calm. Her voice was just a little tremulous at first, perhaps. She seemed shy and embarrassed all the evening, and for the first time since they had come to know each other both Gilmour and she had little to say. They neither of them made the slightest reference to the events of the morning—not until they were about to separate for the night, and then Kate said, as she stood at the doorway of her hut, holding Gilmour's hand in hers—

" We shall be brother and sister always, Tom— always—shan't we ? "

And Gilmour bowed his head, and silently accepted his fate.

CHAPTER XVII.

As yet Gilmour was still unable to see his way to continue the flight across the Njiri plain back to Kilimanjaro, although every day it became increasingly evident that something must be done, and that speedily.

The Masai herdsmen, forced by the failure of the grass crops on the plains, were daily encroaching more and more on the mountain pasturage, rendering the position of the little party of fugitives proportionately insecure. Food, too, was becoming more scarce. The little stock of provisions so thoughtfully brought from Pepo-ni was fast running low, and the proximity of the Masai restricted all trapping or shooting operations to an extremely narrow area.

And now, to further enhance the uneasiness of the situation, Gilmour's too hasty avowal had raised a feeling of embarrassment between himself and Kate, which they could neither of them overcome. Try as they would to meet each other on the old frank footing, there was always in their minds the uneasy sense of a topic on which between them there must be silence.

Kate, in particular, with her frequent doubts as to what her feelings towards Gilmour really were, or rather her inability to read those feelings aright, felt shy and awkward. Her usual sprightliness of manner disappeared, though, for Gilmour's sake, she endeavoured in his presence to assume a cheerfulness she did not feel.

Gilmour was not to be deceived. He saw too well that Kate was restless and unhappy. Frequently her face showed traces of secret tears, and sometimes when they were sitting together talking her eyes would suddenly fill, and in the middle of a sentence, perhaps, she would break off and relapse into pensive silence. Then, with aching heart, Gilmour would sit and watch her, his love the deeper that it dared not express itself. A thousand times he cursed himself for having raised this tangible, though unacknowledged, barrier between them, and ardently he longed for the hour when the continuance of their flight would give them both, in renewed exertion, a respite from their mutual trouble.

The climax came at last. Uledi had been out hunting all morning, and had returned empty-handed. The men looked sullen and dissatisfied, and Gilmour began to fear they might be mutinous. He called them together and held a shauri (palaver) on the situation. While discussing whether it would not be better to risk all and make the attempt to reach Kilimanjaro at once, Resasi, the sentinel for the day, suddenly appeared.

"Habari gani?" (What kind of news) queried Gilmour, sharply.

"They are good," was Resasi's somewhat deliberate reply.

"Allah be praised!" piously exclaimed the Zanzibaris; "Out with them, then," their more practical and impatient master.

"A caravan has arrived going homewards."

"Allah!" "By Jove!" were the characteristic exclamations of the various members of Resasi's audience, each for the moment seeing a speedy end to all their hardships and dangers.

Uledi alone remained silent and moody. Gilmour noted his headman's attitude with a sudden chill of apprehension.

"Well, Uledi, what are your words?" he asked, still trying to look hopeful.

"Bwana, I think Resasi speaks like a fool," was the emphatic and gloomy response.

"Why? Don't you think it would be safe to join the caravan?"

"No. The Masai will come to trade with the caravan. They will demand the bibi back, and you with her. The traders will not dare resist. The bibi will be no longer sacred to them. She will be treated with dishonour, and you will be killed."

Uledi's logic was unanswerable. The men's faces fell; Gilmour, too, looked downcast.

"I suppose we must just wait on, then," he said dejectedly.

"No, that is the worst of it; we cannot wait on. The el-moruū will tell the Wa-Swahili the manner of Ngai's flight. The traders will laugh at them, and explain how it was done. Then they will vow vengeance. They will hunt us down, and——"

"And?"

"We shall all be killed."

This was a terrible damper to the men's newly raised hopes. Not one of them had a sanguine word to say in reply. Gilmour simply accepted the situation.

"We must go at once, then," he said.

"Not before the moon rises in the early morning, Bwana," said Uledi. "It will be time enough then."

"All right. Get everything in order now;" and Gilmour turned away to apprise Kate of the fresh complication, and bid her prepare for flight.

When he returned to his men, he found them making their preparations in a dejected, half-hearted way, which filled him with a vague fear that they might be meditating desertion to the caravan. It was some consolation, however, to see Resasi, usually the most cowardly and lazy, now all energy and action. He seemed to laugh at the coming dangers, and at his companions for appearing to dread them.

What orders he had to give, Gilmour spoke in a kindly, cheerful tone that had the effect of arousing his men somewhat from their apathy. By-and-by they set to work with a will, and by sunset Gilmour had the satisfaction of seeing all his arrangements completed, the greatly diminished loads tied and laid ready for lifting, and every one apparently disposed to face their difficulties with a stout heart.

As usual, Ulu seemed quite elated by the present little extra excitement, and the prospect of more ; while Kate, now that the moment of departure had all but come, did not know whether to be glad or sorry. But for the trouble of these last few days she and Gilmour had been very happy together ; and now that they were about definitely to begin their homeward journey, for the first time the possibility of their future separation began to dawn upon her. She had become so accustomed to his companionship, so used to rely on him for everything, that she could scarcely imagine what her life had ever been or would ever be without him. She would be glad to be home again, glad to see her father; but, then, to have to say good-bye to Tom—ah, how was she going to bring herself to face that?

Some such thought it was which brought the tears to her eyes as she bade Gilmour good-night, and kept her awake long after all the others had gone to rest. Gilmour, too, was wakeful; he, too, was wondering what life would be like without the girl who had grown so dear to him. More immediate, however, was the thought of securing her safety, and how it was to be accomplished. It seemed to Gilmour that he had scarcely fallen asleep when he was aroused by the voice of Uledi.

"Bwana, Bwana," whispered the headman, hurriedly.

"Yes. What is it? Is it time to go?" asked Gilmour, wide awake in an instant.

"Yes. Be quick. Resasi has run away."

"Run away!" repeated Gilmour, in a horrified tone, as he started to his feet. "And the others?"

"We are here, Bwana," cried the men, replying for themselves from the door of the hut.

Gilmour uttered an exclamation of relief. "Is everything ready?"

"Yes."

"Then up with your bundles. I shall go and wake the bibi. By-the-by, don't tell her about Resasi; it would only frighten her."

"Too late, Tom. The bibi knows already," said that young lady herself, smiling a little as she joined the group, and gently laid her hand on Gilmour's shoulder.

In the dim light of the dying camp-fire, Kate could see that Gilmour looked slightly taken aback. He had not noticed her emerge from her hut, and thought that she would be still asleep.

"Now, don't look alarmed," Kate went on; "I am not a bit frightened. Is it time to go?"

Gilmour looked at her. At that moment Kate seemed more calm and collected than any of them.

"Yes," he said, "if you are ready."

"Quite ready."

"Come along, then."

In deep darkness they began groping their way down the precipitous face of the mountain. Without other accident than an occasional slip, or the alarm caused by the noise of the stones their steps sometimes sent rolling down the steep slope, they reached the bottom. Assisted by the night fires of the traders' camp, they were able to judge of their exact position, and steer clear of the Masai kraals, so that soon they were outside the circle of immediate danger.

It being altogether impossible to attempt the direct passage of the Njiri desert, there was nothing for it but to take a long, circuitous route by the Lingerinning Hills, which, besides being out of the usual road of caravans or Masai raiders, had the further advantage of lying largely through stunted forest.

The progress of the little party was necessarily slow, and subject to the usual African night alarms; but the darkness passed without any disagreeable incident of a serious nature.

At daybreak the fugitives remarked with satisfaction that they were already at a considerable distance from Dónyo Erók. With rising hopes of passing unmolested, they found the country utterly parched, and showing no evidence of having been recently occupied by the Masai. Nor were their hopes belied, for during all that day the only signs of inhabitants they met with were deserted kraals and disused cattle-tracks. So great was their feeling of security that, during the heat of the day, a halt was made in order to allow Kate to recover somewhat after her fatiguing march. At the same time, Uledi was fortunate enough to bring down a fine gazelle with his bow and arrow, a most welcome acquisition to them in their half-starved condition. What they did not use at once was cut into strips, and partly smoked and dried over the fire, to be carried with them for a future occasion.

Resuming their tramp in the afternoon, they reached the Lingerinning Hills at sunset, to find them, to their intense satisfaction, likewise deserted. Next day the Njiri desert must be crossed, and here came the most trying part of their journey. It would be little short of a miracle if they could traverse that wide, sandy plain unseen. Their chief hope lay in reaching a small rocky hill which rose midway in the flat expanse of shining sand. If they could but manage that, they would be comparatively safe. Everything depended on that *if*, however.

The first part of the day's march lay through open bushland, and was safely and easily accomplished, the midday heat being again avoided by a three hours' halt under a group of shady bushes. Early in the afternoon our travellers reached the edge of the sheltering strip of covered land, and before them stretched the dreary waste, from which the air rose as from heated metal. So flat and even was the sandy surface, so utterly devoid of rock or tree, that every square yard could be seen as clearly as along the glassy surface of a lake.

Long and anxiously did Gilmour and his handful of men scan the monotonous landscape. Not a human being was to be descried, not a living creature even, save one or two antelopes and zebras moving leisurely about, or pausing to crop the scanty herbage. The little party breathed more freely, and regarded each other with brightened faces as they hopefully resumed their march. Silently they tramped along in single file, the crunching of the sand under their feet alone breaking the stillness. Ever as they went their eyes sharply swept the horizon; but no cause of alarm was to be discovered, no enemy appeared.

The sun began to sink in the western sky, surrounded by its halo of evening glory. The sweltering heat and dazzling glare gradually abated. A cool breeze swept gently over the land, and fanned the dusty, travel-stained faces of the fugitives. Another hour would bring them to the hill, and next day they would be out of Masai-land.

The excitement grew less intense. Already Gilmour felt as if they were safe, and began to talk lightly and cheerfully with Kate, complimenting her on her walking powers. Suddenly Uledi stopped short.

"Hullo! What's up?" queried Gilmour, stopping likewise, and interrupting himself in the middle of a sentence.

For a moment Uledi made no reply, but stood as if deaf, a look of inquietude on his face, his eyes riveted on some distant object. Every one halted, alarmed by these signs of doubt. The eagle eye of Uledi was known to be rarely at fault.

"Bwana," he said at last, extending his muscular arm towards the north-west, "do you see nothing *there ?*"

Gilmour strained his eyes in the direction indicated, but could at first see nothing.

"Yes," he said at length, after a further anxious scrutiny; "I do see something—some dust, I think, raised by the wind."

"Look again, Bwana. See, something moves."

"By Jove, yes! There are zebras galloping away as if frightened. What can have—— Good God! there are spears! The Masai are after us."

Dumb with horror, Gilmour looked mechanically at Kate, and from Kate to the still distant hill. How was she to reach it before the Masai were upon them?

"Look, Bwana, you can see them plainly now," cried Uledi. "There are at least twenty. They see us, for they run."

"We must run too, then," cried Gilmour. "Quick, Kate! give me your hand. Uledi, you take the other. Now, then, all of you—to the hill as fast as you can."

The pursued had three miles to cover, the pursuers six; but on the one side was a half-exhausted, delicately nurtured girl, on the other

brawny savages, inured to exertion and physical
endurance. Quickly the distance between the two
parties was lessened; slowly—oh, so slowly—that
between the fugitives and the hill.

Dragged along by Gilmour and Uledi, Kate had
covered two miles, the warriors four and a half.
There was only half a mile between them now,
and steadily—not running their best—the Masai
were lessening the interval. Another few minutes
of desperate effort on Kate's part, and still half a
mile lay between her and safety; only a quarter
between her and those gleaming spears. She
seemed ready to drop. Time must be gained
somehow, or all would be lost.

"Ferhani, take the bibi's arm," cried Gilmour.

"Tom, what is it? What are you going to do?"
gasped Kate, nervously, retaining her grasp of
Gilmour's hand, as she divined he was about to
attempt something dangerous.

Gilmour returned no answer. "Run on," he
said; "it's all right. Ferhani, why do you stand?"
he shouted savagely to the negro, who stood gazing
at him stupidly, half paralyzed with fear.

Kate was too much exhausted to resist. Blindly
she allowed herself to be hurried along by Tubu
and Ferhani, her heart filled with a sickening dread
for Gilmour that deprived her of all other consciousness.

Gilmour, meanwhile, made good his opportunity. "Now, Uledi," he said, "we must try to stop them."

In a twinkling his rifle was at his shoulder. Loud and clear the crack rang over the silent desert, and down sank a warrior dead or dying. For a moment the Masai stopped, amazed at the result of a shot at what seemed to them such an impossible distance. As they gathered round the fallen man and discovered the wound, they raised an excited cry of wonder, which speedily changed into a shout of vengeance.

Gilmour and Uledi stood motionless. Their object was to gain time, not to slaughter human beings. Resting their guns on the ground, they stood at ease to recover nerve and breath. Once or twice they turned their heads to mark the progress of the three fugitives.

On came the el-moran once more. With savage whoop and brandished spear, they bore down on their expected victims. Five hundred yards—four hundred—three hundred, were quickly passed. Once more it was time for Gilmour to act.

"Now, Uledi," he cried; and at the signal up went both their rifles.

Even as the hammers fell, there was a cry from the lytunu. The warriors sank flat on the ground, and both bullets went ricochetting harmlessly over the plain. Characteristic exclamations burst from master and man, as, with a shout of triumph, the Masai immediately sprang to their feet. But the exultant savages had reckoned without their host. They had yet to learn the value of a double-barrelled, breech-loading rifle. Scarcely had they regained their footing on the slippery sand, when "bang! bang!" went the rifles again, and two more warriors rolled over. On came the rest, secure that now their opponents were at their mercy.

In a twinkling the rifles were reloaded, and again raised deliberately to the shoulder. As before, the Masai threw themselves on the ground.

But Gilmour and Uledi were not to be caught twice, and they lowered their weapons without firing. Surprised at the silence, the el-moran lay for a moment awaiting the expected discharge. None came, and, ordered by their leader, up they sprang. Immediately the watchful pair took aim, and one more warrior remained behind. The rest halted in dismay, with manifest inclination to retire. Still it seemed disgraceful that they, Masai el-moran, should be held at bay by two men, whoever they might be. Stung by the thought, the lytunu rushed madly forward, and, encouraging each other with ferocious cries, the rest followed.

Again the same tricks were tried on both sides, always to the advantage of the defenders. The warriors, however, were now perilously near; another rush, and it would be a hand-to-hand encounter. Gilmour glanced hastily round. To his delight, he saw that Kate had all but gained the hill.

"Run, Uledi," he cried, as once more the disappointed savages started up in pursuit. "Don't fire; save your ammunition."

A yell of delight broke from their pursuers as the two turned and fled. In the loose sand Gilmour found himself heavily handicapped with his big European boots; but he had plenty of "go" and determination in him, and he kept on bravely. Slowly and surely, however, the Masai began to gain ground. Uledi could easily have kept ahead, but, with rare devotion, he ran side by side with his master. Matters began to look serious. Evidently before Gilmour could reach the hill the Masai would be upon him.

"Leave me, Uledi," he gasped, fully alive to his peril. "You must look after the bibi."

But Uledi apparently was deaf. What was the bibi to him? He only knew his master.

"Go on, Uledi, go on," Gilmour urged again.

But still Uledi paid no heed, and kept his even pace.

At that moment Kate reached the hill, and disappeared among its rocks and bushes. Gilmour had still a hundred yards to run; twenty only separated him from his pursuers. Every nerve and muscle was strained to the utmost; still the Masai gained. The respective distances became forty and ten. Gilmour felt himself giving way. He looked round, stumbled, and nearly fell. A yell of triumph burst from the advancing savages. With uplifted spear the leader rushed forward. Uledi stopped and fired. The Masai fell, shot through the heart. Steadying himself on his knees, Gilmour also fired, and cut short the race of the second man. Wild with rage, the others came on in full cry.

The rifles of Gilmour and Uledi were now empty. They threw them aside, and drew their revolvers, resolved to die like men. Another moment, and the unequal contest would have commenced; but just as Gilmour fired his revolver, its feeble report was drowned in a rifle discharge from the bushes. This was more than the Masai had bargained for. Panic-stricken, they turned, and took refuge behind a neighbouring rock, leaving Gilmour and Uledi to pick up their rifles and stagger forward to the temporary safety of the hill, as the sun sank below the horizon.

CHAPTER XVIII.

THE position of Gilmour and his little party was now desperate. As they gathered together in a little hollow among the rocks, their eyes looked the question they none of them dared utter. What was to become of them now? There was a dead silence.

Gilmour was the first to speak. "Ferhani," he said, "you keep a look-out. The Masai may surprise us."

"Eh wallah, Bwana!" and Ferhani took up his position on an outstanding rock.

Again there was silence. Once more it was broken by Gilmour.

"Well, what's to be done now?" he asked.

No one spoke.

"Will they attack us again to-night?" Gilmour went on, turning towards Uledi.

"No, Bwana; I think not. They have had too sharp a lesson."

There was a general sigh of relief; it was a comfort to know they were to have some respite, however brief.

"What do you think they'll do, then?" was Gilmour's next question.

"Wait for help probably. Already the firing may have been heard by distant Masai, or they may have sent for reinforcements. In the morning we may have to face a hundred instead of fourteen."

"But why wait till morning?" interposed Kate, energetically. "Can't we fly during the night?"

Gilmour shook his head. "The moment the Masai saw we were gone, they would be after us, and in the darkness we should have a very poor chance. Besides, how could you walk any further to-night?"

"Oh, I think I could manage if——"

"Bwana," interrupted Uledi, "do you know that we have very little ammunition?"

Gilmour started. "Very little ammunition! How much?" he asked sharply.

Immediately the pouches were overhauled. To every one's dismay, they were found to contain not more than six rounds each, with about double that number for the revolvers. This was the worst discovery yet made, and the fugitives sat gazing at each other in silent consternation.

"There's nothing for it but to risk a night

flight," said Kate at last. "We could hold our own against fourteen; but if there are fifty in the morning, we should have no chance."

Still there was silence. With their wider experience of the difficulty of fighting under such circumstances, and their more accurate knowledge of the dangers of savage warfare, the men could not so readily snatch at the grain of hope held out to them in Kate's suggestion.

"Don't you think so, Tom?" she asked, after a pause.

"Yes, it's our only hope—a very poor one, too," said Gilmour, despairingly. "We can't all go, though," he added slowly, apparently talking to himself.

"Can't all go?" repeated Kate. "What do you mean?"

"I mean that one of us must stay all night on that rock in sight of the Masai. As long as they see some one there, they will think they have us all safe under their eye, and will make up their minds to let us alone till morning."

"And what will become of the man who stays?" asked Kate, in blank bewilderment. "Why, Tom," she gasped, slowly beginning to grasp the full meaning of the proposal when Gilmour made no reply, "he will—he will be killed!"

"Oh no," said Gilmour, speaking with affected

cheerfulness; "he can run for his life in the morning."

But Kate was not to be so put off. "Oh, Tom, you know very well he wouldn't have the smallest chance," she said reproachfully. "You *couldn't* leave any of your men in such a horrible position."

"No, I couldn't do that," was the decided answer, spoken in a low tone of stern determination.

"I knew it," exclaimed Kate, greatly relieved. "Then, we shall all go together, shan't we?"

Gilmour looked very grave. "No, Kate; it is impossible," he said.

"Then, what do you mean? What are we to do?" cried Kate, in renewed alarm.

"I shall remain myself."

"Tom!" Words cannot describe the accent of horrified amazement with which Kate gasped out that one brief monosyllable, nor the wild pang of agonized terror that shot through her heart as the fearful meaning of Gilmour's words flashed itself into her brain. For the second time in her life, she seemed about to faint. Her head swam; a strange mist gathered before her eyes. She swayed, and would have fallen but for Gilmour's supporting arm.

"Kate, there is nothing else for it," Gilmour went on tremulously, deeply affected by her agitation.

Kate drew herself together, and opened her eyes with a little shiver. "Hush, Tom, hush!" she entreated, clasping her hands to stay their nervous trembling.

But Gilmour paid no heed to the whispered remonstrance. "You must go and lie down now," he went on with greater firmness. "You will need all your strength for the journey you have before you. Before midnight you must leave here with Ulu and the men."

Again Kate shivered, but otherwise she made no sign of having heard. Gilmour gently laid his hand upon hers; it was cold as ice. For a moment he bent over her with pitying eyes, his heart burning with the desire to clasp her in his arms. It was hard—oh, so hard!—to see the loved one suffering thus, and yet not dare to offer what of solace love could give. Ah, if she had only loved him in return, how much easier in one way it would have been for both! and yet, in another, how much harder!—harder to say good-bye, harder to part, harder—ah, so very much harder!—to have to relinquish each other for ever.

For ever? Yes, it would be for ever. Gilmour had no hope of seeing Kate again, once they had said good-bye to each other now. Still, he remembered through all the agony of that thought, that to let Kate know the truth would only be to seal the fate of both of them. Her generous nature would never deliberately accept the sacrifice of his life for hers, he knew; never agree to any proposal that did not seem to leave him some loophole of escape. Accordingly, when he resumed, it was in a voice that showed no trace of the feelings which agitated him.

"You should reach the other side of the plain by daylight; and once at the mountain, you are practically safe. Don't trouble yourself too much about me. At daybreak I shall slip away and make a run for it, and I'll back myself to run against any Masai among them. Besides, I have *this* to stop them, if they give chase;" and Gilmour significantly tapped the handle of his revolver.

Kate let him go on to the end in silence. When he had finished, she confronted him calmly for a moment, her cheeks pale, her lips closely compressed.

"Tom, I will *not* go," she said, in a low clear tone of firm resolution. "I cannot allow you to throw away your life for me. If you stay, I stay. We must take our chance together."

Gilmour could make no reply. For the time he was astounded, overwhelmed, at the calm decision of Kate's voice and bearing. If she had wept, or protested, or in any other way displayed the slightest sign of feminine weakness, he would have known how to comfort and persuade. But this unfaltering aspect completely baffled him, and rendered him speechless. Yet never had Gilmour admired Kate more than in that moment when she seemed to set him at defiance; never so keenly felt his love as now, when for the first time he clearly realized of what noble stuff the woman he loved was made.

"What arrangements will you make for passing the night here?" Kate continued, after a pause.

The matter-of-fact question recalled Gilmour to himself, and to a sense of the necessity he and Kate lay under of coming to an immediate understanding.

"Kate, it is impossible. You cannot stay here," he cried emphatically.

Kate's only answer was to look at him with a further tightening of the lips.

"You *must* go to-night," Gilmour went on excitedly. "I tell you there *is* a chance—a chance for a man, but not for a woman."

"I can use a revolver."

"Yes, yes—I know that; but you cannot run as I can. Don't you see that, if I had you to look after, you would only hamper me?"

In the strength of her determination, Kate had forgotten her woman's weakness. She showed signs of wavering.

"Kate, for my sake—as a favour to me," Gilmour urged eagerly—"oh, Kate, you *will* go, won't you?"

For a moment Kate looked at him—looked him full in the face, and read the pleading in his earnest eyes. "Yes, Tom," she began, in a voice that struggled to be calm, "I will do anything——" and then her lip quivered and her eyes fell, and she turned quickly away to hide the tears which choked and blinded her.

Before Gilmour could speak again, Uledi stepped forward.

"Bwana," he said, "you cannot stay alone. I shall stay with you."

"You, Uledi!" cried Gilmour, deeply touched by the faithful fellow's devotion.

"It is God's will," returned Uledi. "Allah has fixed the day of our birth and of our death," he argued, like the pious Mussulman he was.

"But I want you to look after the bibi."

"Ferhani and Tubu will be sufficient."

"You know the risk."

"We cannot flee from our fate," was Uledi's resigned reply.

"It might be for the best," mused Gilmour. "Certainly it would double my chance of escape. Do you hear what Uledi says, Kate?" he asked aloud. "He is going to stay with me. You need have no fear for me now."

Kate looked up gratefully through her tears, then seized Uledi's hand, and shook it warmly. In her gratitude she could have thrown her arms about the man's neck and kissed his black, ugly face. But she restrained herself. As it was, Uledi looked sufficiently embarrassed. Then Kate remembered that this was only a single gleam of light in a whole world of darkness, and her tears flowed anew.

Gilmour looked at her with deep concern. "Kate," he said, laying a kindly hand on her shoulder, "Kate, do try to compose yourself. Remember, you have still a great deal to go through. Come, lie down now and rest a little;" and, without waiting for a reply, Gilmour, as well as he could, set about arranging a place for her among the stones.

Half stupefied with grief, Kate allowed herself to be led to it, and unresistingly lay down as Gilmour bade her. With a final injunction that she should try to go to sleep, Gilmour left her and set about making the last arrangements for the coming flight. He tried hard to get Uledi to accompany Kate, and leave Ferhani with him; but the man turned a deaf ear to all his persuasions, and reluctantly Gilmour had to yield. He was just about to give his directions to Ferhani when Ulu timidly approached.

"May I stay too, Bwana?" she asked.

"Good gracious, no!" was Gilmour's rather sharp reply. "You would only be in the way, you know," he added more gently. "Besides, the bibi will want you."

"I do not know the bibi," urged Ulu; "you are my master."

"But I don't want my little mtoto to be killed. You must go with the others."

Ulu did not argue or remonstrate further. She had not become sufficiently like the wives of the white men for that; but in her own mind she made her own resolves. Without another word she withdrew, leaving Gilmour overwhelmed by this fresh proof of the girl's affection for him.

Other and less pleasant subjects demanded his attention, however, and Gilmour turned to Tubu and Ferhani to give such orders as occurred to him for Kate's safe conduct across the desert, and back through Chaga to the mission station. In a jerky fashion he continued his conversation with the men as long as he could, talking in a low, subdued voice, so as, if possible, not to disturb Kate. He had need of some distraction to stave off the gloomy thoughts which threatened to master and unman him. Time after time he enjoined Tubu and Ferhani to guard the bibi like an angel of Allah, and as they hoped for a place in paradise;

and it afforded him a certain satisfaction to hear them swear by the beard of Mohammed that, please God, she should be safely handed over to the malaam, her father.

As Kate lay on the hard ground close by, she heard frequent snatches of the conversation. Every earnest word of deep solicitude thrilled her with a new pang. Worn and weary as she was, she could not sleep. The memory of all Gilmour had done for her, the thought of all he was about to do, tortured and maddened her. How brave, how good, how generous he was! and—how he loved her! Why could she not love him in return? *Did* she not love him in return? This anguish of heart at the thought of parting, this feeling that to stay with him and die would be easier than to leave him and live—surely it was the outcome of something deeper than gratitude and mere sisterly liking? Yes, she was sure of it; she had made a mistake; she would go to him and tell him so, and claim love's right to live or die with him.

But why should she be tortured with such doubts? All the people she had ever heard or read of seemed to be able to distinguish quite clearly between love and friendship, and she—she could not, even now. Was it that her friendship was stronger or her love weaker than the friendship and love of others, or was she even justified

in calling by the name of love this feeling which in
her seemed but friendship intensified? Surely
there must be about love some visible mark that
from its birth would stamp it with a peculiar
sanctity? And yet, for her part, Kate could distinguish none. Best be silent, therefore, lest she
should be deceiving herself, lest the desire to repay
one debt should engender another too great for her
to meet.

Again and again Kate was driven from one conclusion to the other, until, at length, she could do
battle with her doubts no longer—there seemed to
be no solution of them. She must think of something else, speak to some one to keep her from
thinking.

> " ' Oh, the little more, and how much it is,
> And the little less, and what worlds away!' "

she sighed, as she wearily sat up, and scrambled
painfully to her feet. At the sound of her footsteps
approaching the place where he sat, Gilmour turned
quickly round.

"Now, Kate, this is too bad," he began reproachfully.

"Oh, Tom, don't! I couldn't bear it any longer.
It's no good trying to go to sleep—I can't. Do let
me sit beside you and talk to you."

It did not need Kate's tone of urgent entreaty to
make Gilmour yield to her desire. He was only

too glad in this last hour together to have her as near him as possible. Silently he made a place for her by his side, and hand-in-hand they sat in the starlight, not talking much, but seemingly understanding each other better than ever before. Gradually a subdued feeling of pleasure and contentment stole over both, and they sank into silence. Kate closed her eyes and leaned her head against Gilmour's arm. She seemed to be asleep.

But the moment of parting had come. Half an hour more, and the moon would be up; the fugitives must be some distance from the hill ere its betraying light flooded the surrounding plain. Fortunately the night had become somewhat cloudy, and earnestly Gilmour hoped that the cloudiness would continue. Tenderly he bent over Kate, unwilling to disturb her. It was so hard to have to wake her, so hard to tell her she must go. He took one long, silent, lingering look.

"Kate," he whispered softly at last, almost hoping that the sound of his voice would not reach her ears.

Kate opened her eyes. "Yes, Tom," she said.

"The moon will soon be up. It is time to go."

Kate shivered and closed her eyes again. For some moments she lay quite still.

"Come, Kate," urged Gilmour again; "there is no time to lose."

Kate looked up at him mutely, uncomprehendingly. Then she seemed to remember, and staggered blindly to her feet. Gilmour gave her his hand. She clung to it wildly with both hers.

"Oh, Tom, I cannot, *cannot* bear to leave you," she cried, in a broken voice.

Gilmour dared not trust himself to speak; his emotion choked and blinded him. Silently he returned Kate's passionate hand-clasp.

"Good-bye, Kate," he stammered at length; "good-bye."

Kate only tightened her grasp; she could not utter a word. A wild impulse seized her to throw her arms about Gilmour's neck and tell him that she loved him with her whole heart and soul; but some hidden motive held her back.

"Good-bye, Kate," Gilmour again murmured brokenly, making as if he would lead her away.

Kate held him fast. "Oh, Tom! dear Tom!" she managed to say amid her choking sobs, and, stooping down, she carried his hand to her lips and covered it with passionate kisses. Suddenly she let go her hold, and, not daring to look up, she turned swiftly away and set her face towards the dreary wilderness of Njiri.

"Ferhani, look after the bibi," were the last tremulous words Kate heard, as she staggered blindly forward into the starlit darkness.

With a warm pressure of the hand and a low
" kwahéri," Gilmour took leave of Ulu and Tubu;
then he sat down on a rock, and through the tears
which would not be restrained he sorrowfully
watched Kate descending the hill. On reaching
the entrance of a dry nullah she turned and looked
up towards him. Gilmour detected a waving
handkerchief. He waved his own in return, and
then—then the darkness closed over her, and Kate
was lost to his sight for ever.

A few minutes later, the moon rose from behind
the Kyubu Mountains, and shed its mystic light
over the dreary landscape. The desolate watcher
strained his eyes, if possible to catch another
glimpse of the dear one. In vain. Kate was seen
no more. " God protect and support her," was
her lover's silent prayer.

In the midst of Gilmour's grief Uledi came to
him. With all the eloquence at his command the
man urged his master to take a little rest in preparation for the trials of the morrow. At first
Gilmour would not listen, but as he became more
calm he recognized the justice of what Uledi said,
and yielded at length to his servant's urgent
solicitations. Stretching himself out, Gilmour,
more fortunate than Kate, soon fell into a peaceful
sleep, utterly worn out by the mental and physical
strain of the last twelve hours.

And statuesque Uledi sat upon a rock, guarding the white man's slumber, while below lay the wakeful Masai, keeping eager watch lest their prey should escape them.

CHAPTER XIX.

MEN situated like Gilmour sleep but lightly. About two in the morning, aroused by some slight sound, he suddenly awoke. Uledi was still on the watch, but not alone. Gilmour rubbed his eyes, unable to credit the evidence of his senses. There sat Ulu, keeping Uledi company! He started up in alarm. Could some accident have befallen Kate?

"Ulu!" he cried, after a moment's pause, "where is the bibi?"

Ulu jumped to her feet with a guilty start, conscious of having disobeyed her master, afraid of the consequences, yet glorying in what she had done.

"The bibi is safe, Bwana," she stammered.

"Then why have you left her?" Gilmour asked, his fear turned to intense astonishment.

"Because I belong to you. I shall help you to fight the Masai."

Gilmour was silent. Much as he regretted her

return, he could not help being touched by the girl's devoted attachment. For a moment the thought crossed his mind, " What shall I do with her, if ever I get out of this confounded trap ? " But the question was one which it was yet premature to discuss, and he dismissed it with an expressive shrug of the shoulders.

Then Ulu told how she had managed to run away. She had only accompanied Kate as far as the end of the nullah, then, seizing her opportunity, had slipped away. After remaining in hiding for an hour, she retraced her steps, and narrowly escaped being shot by Uledi for a Masai, as she approached the rock on which he kept guard.

With some difficulty, Gilmour now succeeded in persuading Uledi to allow him to take his place, and bade the man lie down for an hour or two's well-earned rest.

The scene which lay outspread before him as he sat upon the rock, Ulu lying at his feet like a faithful dog, was one which accorded well with Gilmour's present state of gloomy foreboding. Beyond and below him stretched the flat, unbroken expanse of Njiri, with here and there a bank of fog hanging over it, shining weird and ghost-like under the fitful rays of the moon. The air resounded with the melancholy cry of night-jars and

owls, the strange whistle of zebras, the moan of
buffaloes, and the distant roar of lions. To the
south rose grim and dark the sombre majesty of
Kilimanjaro; overhead glittered its snowy crown,
projected against the starlit sky like a bright
cloud of exceeding whiteness. To the east, the
mountains of Kyubu were faintly outlined through
the silvery haze. The atmosphere seemed heavy
with the presentiment of impending evil.

But Gilmour thought little of it. With eyes
riveted on the Masai spear-heads glittering in the
moonlight, he sat pensive and motionless, while
unnoted the twinkling stars silently moved westward, their course telling of the passing night.

The thoughts which occupied Gilmour's mind
were melancholy enough in all conscience. As he
sat with elbow resting on knee, and hand supporting head, it was in the full knowledge that he had
to prepare for death. Often and often he had told
himself before, and now sadly told himself again,
that if, indeed, he had to die, he would only be
leaving a world he was not in harmony with—a
world that to him had been one great disappointment. What had he to look forward to but disappointment greater still? With Kate life might
have been different. With her to help him he
might yet have been able to find some meaning
in the tangled maze, some happiness, some satis-

faction in the world. As it was, to die for her was better than to live without her.

And yet—it was hard to die. Face to face with death men gain a clearer insight into the value of life, and even in that moment of despairing acquiescence in his impending fate, Gilmour, in the pride of his strength and manhood, felt that life was very, very dear. Something seemed to whisper to him, too, that Kate had been mistaken—that love already lurked within her heart, though by her as yet an unacknowledged presence. What a prospect of bliss that thought opened up to him —what anguish that it should meet him at the side of a yawning grave.

At times Gilmour's fancy wandered to Kate herself, one by one recalling her well-loved features, or following her in her weary tramp over the desert. It was a relief to think of her progress towards life and liberty, a comfort to know that though there might be no one else in the world to cherish his memory, to her, at least, it would be ever sacred.

Meanwhile the night wore on. The moon had long since crossed the zenith ; the air grew sharper and more cold. Slowly the fog-banks spread across the plain, creeping mysteriously towards the hill, and threatening to enfold it in their damp embrace. Everything betokened the approach of morning.

With a start Gilmour roused himself from his gloomy reverie. He glanced quickly at the sky; then his eye noted the approaching fog-banks, and across his mind flashed the thought that these misty wreaths would give the enemy a terrible advantage, by acting as a screen to hide their movements.

"Uledi! Uledi!" he cried. In an instant the Zanzibari was at his side. "Look."

"Allah!" Uledi took in the situation at a glance. There was nothing more said. Both understood the fearful significance of the approaching fog-banks; both foresaw that the coming combat would be short and sharp, and a hundred times more dangerous than even their worst fears had anticipated.

"Uledi," said Gilmour, breaking the silence, "we will show them how we can fight and how we can die."

"Yes, by Allah! and that we will not die alone."

Then, instinctively, the two men looked at their rifles and ammunition, and saw that their revolvers were ready for action. Another horrible interval of waiting and inaction followed. Silent the watchers sat, their rifles lying across their knees, eye and ear on the alert for the first sign of movement on the part of the enemy. Slowly, almost imperceptibly, the mist came creeping on and around them—the cold, grey mist, that for aught they knew might be their shroud; nearer and ever nearer, till at last the hill looked like a rocky island lapped around by silvery waters. Helpless, despairing, like shipwrecked mariners, Gilmour and Uledi sat watching the ever-rising tide, with no means of escape before them—no distant sail on the horizon—only the one dread certainty of slowly approaching doom.

Smaller and smaller grew the hill; nearer and nearer drew the bank of fog, in whose fleecy folds lurked bloody, violent death. It reached the place where lay the Masai, but before it had altogether enveloped them the warriors had grasped their shields and plucked their spears from the ground. Gilmour and Uledi looked at each other significantly. Neither spoke, but with clenched teeth and nervous hands they sat fingering their weapons, ready for instant action. At any moment now the Masai war-cry might sound in their ears, and the hidden enemy be upon them. It behoved them to make their final dispositions.

"You, Ulu, lie behind that rock and watch towards the south; you, Uledi, keep a look-out to the east and north. I'll look after the rest."

Gilmour's whispered orders were at once obeyed, and silently each took the post assigned.

Again there was a pause. The hearts of the

watchers beat audibly. The suspense was enough
to age a man ten years in as many minutes.
Gradually the pale moonlight faded before the
breaking day, a faint flicker of hope springing up
with the approach of morning.

At length, vaguely outlined in the mist, appeared
the figure of a warrior, creeping, cat-like, from
rock to rock. Immediately Gilmour fired, and
amid the multitudinous echoes which followed, he
heard an exclamation and a cry of pain. A dozen
Masai rushed forward. To their surprise and
dismay they found themselves out of the sheltering
mist. Bang, bang! went the rifles of Gilmour and
Uledi. Unprepared for such a reception, the
warriors faltered a moment, then rushed backward
into the mist again.

With nervous haste the rifles were reloaded; the
next attack would be more fierce and deadly. Foot
by foot the upper portion of the hill became
enshrouded; the clear area grew smaller and
smaller. At length the little trio were completely
enveloped—the cold, damp fog was all around
and above them. At ten yards' distance objects
were only vaguely discernible, and eyes were
despairingly strained in the direction of the looked-
for advance, expectant each moment of cold blue
steel and ferocious faces.

The end came at last. Suddenly, from behind

looming bush and rock, the bloodthirsty savages leaped into view, looking through the haze more like demons than men. Blood-curdling shouts filled the air, now gleaming with the wicked glitter of uplifted spears.

With a wild war-whoop Uledi sprang to his feet. Simultaneously he and Gilmour discharged the four barrels of their rifles with deadly effect. Groans and cries of pain mingled horribly with the clash of spears and shouts of battle.

There was no time to reload. Casting their rifles aside, the attacked drew their revolvers. Crack, crack, crack! they went in rapid succession. At every shot a warrior fell dead or dying. All the foremost of the band were already down. Those in the rear wavered, uncertain whether to advance or retire. Gilmour took advantage of their hesitation to rush forward and seize the shield of one of their fallen comrades. The action roused their wrath, and inspired them with fresh courage. Once more they darted forward, shouting their incentive cries. There must be no more wavering. Victory or death was the alternative in each man's thoughts.

Holding the captured shield in his left hand, Gilmour again fired his revolver, and two more warriors dropped out of the fray. Next moment the rest were close upon him. A third time he

touched the trigger. There was no report. With
frantic energy he pulled and pulled. In vain—the
revolver was empty! With a fierce exclamation,
he dashed the useless weapon to the ground.
There was a sudden onrush of Masai. Something
from behind struck Gilmour in the thigh. He was
aware of a sharp, stinging pain. A horrible
sickness seized him; his head swam; spears
glittered murderously before his eyes. Then all
was oblivion, as he sank unconscious to the
ground, his body half covered by the shield he still
firmly grasped.

Meanwhile, a smaller number had set upon
Uledi, only to meet a yet more deadly reception.
Every man fell dead or wounded before his rapid
and unerring aim. With a wild caper, and a
whoop of savage triumph, the M-Swahili turned
to help his master. He was just in time to see
three warriors rushing upon Gilmour full tilt, while
a fourth poised his spear to deal a deadly blow
from behind. Ere the stroke descended, there was
a puff of smoke from the rock behind which lay
Ulu. The warrior staggered forward, and the
spear, intended for Gilmour's heart, glanced harmlessly off a projecting rock which he struck as
he fell. Simultaneously Uledi fired; and now
there remained only two Masai to deal with. Well
might Uledi, as they turned upon him, call aloud

to Allah and Mohammed! When he pulled the trigger, his revolver, like Gilmour's, was silent! Promptly he drew back his hand, and, with a fierce imprecation, dashed the weapon in the face of his advancing foe. The Masai fell brained. With the agility of a cat, Uledi dodged the spear of the dead man's companion. Then, like a savage gladiator, he bided his time. Again his assailant made a desperate attempt to stab him, and again Uledi dodged. Then, quick as lightning, he sprang at the warrior's throat. Unhappily, he miscalculated —a spear-thrust met him half-way. So great was the impetus of his spring that the weapon went clean through his body, bringing the warrior within his desperate grasp. Thus horribly united, the two rolled over in one last fearful death-grapple, Uledi's fingers almost meeting through his opponent's throat. In that moment of fiercest passion and agony Ulu suddenly emerged from her hiding-place. Without the slightest hesitation, she rushed towards the struggling combatants, and, waiting her opportunity, promptly blew out the brains of the Masai, transfixing in death his distorted face, protruding tongue, and bursting eyeballs. Even as she fired, Uledi's convulsive grip relaxed, and with a horrible laugh of fiendish triumph, which ended in his death-rattle, the faithful Zanzibari fell backwards, dead.

CHAPTER XX.

THERE was silence. Her revolver in her hand, Ulu stood alone in the midst of that scene of dreadful carnage, proud in the consciousness of victory.

Only stopping to assure herself that there were none among the wounded Masai whom she need fear, the girl hastened to where Gilmour lay buried beneath one of the warriors shot by Uledi. With difficulty she succeeded in dragging the yet warm corpse from off her master's body. Anxiously she examined his prostrate form, fearful of discovering some fatal wound. To her relief, she found nothing worse than a spear sticking through his thigh. Her first impulse was to withdraw it, but on second thoughts she decided to leave the weapon where it was. Picking up Gilmour's felt hat, and using it as he himself had done under somewhat similar circumstances, she ran off to a spring at the bottom of the hill. Returning with a supply of water, she dashed some of it on his face, and soon had the satisfaction of seeing her restorative efforts successful.

For some time after regaining consciousness, Gilmour was too dazed to understand the situation. Gradually the recollection of past events returned to him. Looking up with a start, he tried to rise, only to sink back moaning with pain. The memory of the recent battle flashed across his mind.

"Where is Uledi?" he inquired anxiously.

"A-mi-kufa!" (dead) was the laconic response.

Again Gilmour tried to rise, and again he sank back helpless, a groan of grief escaping him as he thought of his faithful servant's heroic devotion.

"Where are the Masai?" he next asked, remembering his own desperate situation.

"Dead too. They are all food for the hyænas."

Had corroboration been wanting, all around lay ghastly enough evidence of the truth of Ulu's statement.

"Bwana," the girl went on, "shall I pull out the spear?"

Slowly and painfully Gilmour raised himself on his elbow. "Stop a moment," he said; "we must see what we are about first. There! Take that handkerchief and tie it above the spear-head. Now put that stick in beneath and twist away as hard as you can. That'll do. Now, out with it!" and Gilmour with difficulty repressed a cry of pain as the huge weapon was promptly withdrawn. "Give the stick another twist," he cried faintly; and for some moments he lay still again, trying to recover himself. In a short time the bleeding ceased, and, after swallowing a little water, he was able to have the wound bandaged up as well as circumstances would permit.

The sun had now risen, and under its influence the mist was rapidly disappearing, revealing the scene of the battle in all its horrible details.

"Where was Uledi killed?" asked Gilmour, sitting up.

Ulu pointed to where the man's dead body lay, half across one of the Masai he had slain.

After a last sorrowful look, Gilmour bade Ulu cover Uledi with branches, and put the largest stones she could move on the top.

"We must not leave him to the hyænas and vultures," he said.

This farewell tribute of respect paid to his dead servant and friend, it behoved Gilmour at once to commence the journey across the desert, though, wounded as he was, there seemed but small hope of his ever reaching Chaga. Partly supported by Ulu, and partly by a stick, he contrived to struggle down to the spring. There he drank long and deeply, not only to assuage his burning thirst, but also in preparation for the journey before him, he having no water-bottle. The desperate tramp for dear life was then begun.

But Gilmour no longer moved forward with the light, springy step of his former vigorous manhood. Slowly and painfully he hobbled along, reduced to dependence on his little negro companion, who for her part stepped out proudly and happily, carrying the gun Gilmour could no longer carry for himself. Ulu's heart beat high as she reflected that not only had she—a mere girl—saved the Bwana's life, but that she had also, with her own hand, killed two Masai el-moran. That, indeed, was a feat which would reflect on her, undying lustre.

As Gilmour trudged on, his wound became less painful, his lameness less pronounced. He began to step out more vigorously. Proportionately, his first feeling of despondency disappeared. Hope of life once more reasserted itself—hope of happiness and love. There was Kate at his journey's end—Kate, who had called him "Dear Tom!" Might he not win her yet? There was inspiration in the very thought. He had something to live for, and he *would* live.

Thus wilfully blinding himself to his desperate situation, Gilmour held bravely on, with growing determination. By this time the sun was well up, and its fierce rays shot through the air with ever-increasing brilliancy and power. From the white, burning sands, the light was reflected in a blinding glare.

Under the combined influence of the heat, the exertion, and the pain of his wound, Gilmour's thirst rapidly returned, and in that God-forgotten expanse of desert there was no place to allay it. His recent confident spirit began to give way. Only by sheer force of will did he keep struggling onward.

And yet the worst had not come. Higher and ever higher rose the blazing sun; more and more pitilessly it beat down upon the weary, wounded, well-nigh exhausted traveller. The air rose in furnace-like blasts around him. His parched tongue clove to the roof of his mouth; the momentary relief afforded by sucking a bullet proved useless. His pace began to slacken; he leaned more heavily on Ulu; now and then he had to stop altogether, in order to recover himself.

Gradually hope faded within him; he would never see Kate again. There was nothing for it but to die—to drag out a slow, horrible, ghastly death of thirst and weakness in the midst of that dreadful desert. Better—better, a thousand times, to have met fate swiftly, at the point of the Masai spears!

And yet—would death be slow? Before the last panting breath had left his tortured body, would not the hyænas be at his throat, the vultures at his eyes?

The thought was maddening, and, with fitful, feverish energy, Gilmour pushed ahead, vainly seeking to shut out the revolting picture.

At length the sun reached the zenith. Overhead, the sky seemed made of brass; around, the atmosphere, like that of an oven, rose quivering and lifelike from the scorching sand.

Gilmour felt himself growing weaker. A feeling of extreme lassitude and oppression seized him, accompanied by splitting headache, and by cramp-like pains in every joint. Alternately, he seemed to burn with heat and shiver with cold. His pulse beat with alarming force and rapidity.

As these unmistakable symptoms of fever developed, his last despairing hope gave way. " God help me now ! " he muttered, " God help me now ! " Then he thought of Ulu. However desperate his own case might be, she still had a chance of life.

" Ulu, leave me ! leave me ! " he entreated. " I can go no further. Never mind me. Save yourself ! "

The girl looked at him wonderingly, with wide-open eyes. Then, as if she had not understood, with all her strength she tried to pull him onwards.

" Come, Bwana," she said, " Come."

" My little mtoto, it's no use. Leave me ! leave me ! "

But Ulu only answered, " Come ! "

" Go," Gilmour urged again ; "go, and be the mtoto of the bibi. Tell her how I died."

" I will not go to the bibi. The bibi left you. Come ! "

Gilmour looked at the girl inquiringly, struck by the tone in which her last words were uttered, and full of wonder at her unflinching devotion. He pressed his point no further, however, and once more staggered forward with slow, faltering steps.

Soon his symptoms changed. Pain and fatigue were felt no longer, and with surprising life and energy he tramped onward through the sand. But it was not now steady plodding towards Chaga, towards the eastern shoulder of Kimawenzi. His movements were jerky, aimless, uncertain. There was a wild, unseeing look in his eyes. As he went along he muttered strangely to himself, or addressed others as if they were present. Gilmour was delirious.

At first Ulu did her best to keep him in the right direction, but it was no use. She was only pushed aside and spoken sharply to in English, which she did not understand. Gilmour no longer recognized his faithful little companion. The events of his past life seemed to be jumbled up perplexingly in his fevered brain. At one moment he was talking earnestly to " Nina," the next he appealed eagerly to Kate. Then it seemed as if Kate and Nina were but two forms of the same person, and he would stop abruptly and stand still for a time, while he painfully tried to unravel the puzzle. Again he would be unable to attach any distinct individuality to Nina. She was merely a creation of his fancy —Kate was the only certainty; and, filled with pleasant thoughts, he would walk quietly on, till once more the idea changed, and Kate seemed a mocking phantom, ever beckoning him towards her, yet ever eluding him.

At times some recollection of recent events crossed his mind, and, greatly to Ulu's danger, Gilmour was once again in fierce combat with the Masai; or he saw himself surrounded by ferocious beasts of prey, met the gleam of their glaring eyeballs, felt their hot breath on his cheek. They were at his throat! they were tearing him to pieces! and with terrible energy he sought to fight the phantom demons, or, seized with ungovernable panic, fled for his life. Up and down Ulu followed him distractedly, ineffectually calling upon him to stop. Then, when the dread hallucination left him, and he dropped exhausted, she would be at his side, urging him, helping him to rise, and perseveringly pulling him towards Chaga.

As the afternoon hours wore on, the worst paroxysm of the fever passed. Gilmour's unnatural energy began to be played out, and exhaustion reasserted itself. He reeled rather than walked; once or twice he fell. Through all his madness raged his agonizing thirst. A consuming fire seemed to be eating its way into his heart. As if to mock him and increase his torments, Nature spread out in the distance what appeared to be limpid sheets of cool, refreshing water. Ever towards them he madly struggled, heedless of Ulu's explanations; but they either flitted on ahead of him, or disappeared as he approached. Sometimes the seeming lakes proved to be gleaming salt reaches, mere efflorescence of the impregnated soil. To Gilmour's fevered eyes, the flake-like crystals seemed as snow, and taking them up in handfuls, he swallowed them eagerly, only to add to his tortures.

The day was fast speeding away, and still the exhausted wayfarers were in the heart of the wilderness. In vain Ulu scanned the horizon for some sign of coming help. There was nothing but the arid waste, in its grim monotony, its stern, pitiless, death-like silence. Succour was hopeless, death inevitable.

The crisis came at last. Gilmour could go no further. His limbs tottered, his head sank forward on his breast. "Water! water!" he feebly gasped, with parched throat and cleaving tongue, as he fell helpless on the ground.

Frantically Ulu pulled and tugged, urging him by voice and action to continue the struggle for life. Useless; he only kept faintly muttering, " Water ! " Move he neither would nor could.

At length Ulu gave up her unavailing efforts. Dazed and overwhelmed, she stood for a moment gazing despairingly at her master. Once more she turned her dust-stained, suffering face towards Kilimanjaro. Grief, hunger, thirst, and fatigue had sadly changed her formerly piquant features. What was she to do ? The Bwana lay at her feet dying. She could be of no further use to him. To save herself she must fly at once, but—— Strong as was the instinct of self-preservation within her, her dog-like devotion to her master was stronger still. Ulu accepted her fate.

Mechanically she sat herself down by Gilmour's side. Gently she raised his head from the burning sand, and with tender solicitude placed it in her lap, so as to shade it from the now almost horizontal rays of the setting sun. Then Ulu waited —waited the approach of death—death for both of them.

The vultures that till now had followed them, wheeling watchfully in mid-air, began to circle downward. With noisy swish they lighted on the few isolated trees which, gaunt and leafless, reared their skeleton forms in the desert. Expectantly the repulsive creatures craned their hideous, feather-less necks, and gloated prospectively over the coming feast. Ulu heeded them not, but with wistful, tearless eyes kept her head bent over Gilmour.

Slowly the sun neared the horizon. For a moment it seemed to linger; then it disappeared. The gold and crimson hues of sunset, which, while they lasted, spoke of life and hope, faded into the dusky tints of evening. From an adjacent mass of rocks a couple of hyænas crawled forth on their nightly search for prey. Inquiringly they held their horrid muzzles in the air, sniffing the evening breeze. Startled by the sudden scent of human beings, like wretched curs they fled instinctively back to the shelter of their lair. Finding them-selves unmolested, and gathering courage with the deepening shades of night, after a time they ven-tured forth again, but watchfully, ready to fly on the slightest alarm. Sighting at last the cause of their primary fears, they began to reconnoitre, circling round at a distance with ungainly trot.

Rapidly the darkness deepened. Still Ulu sat motionless, her head bent close to Gilmour's, her cheek almost touching his. Nearer and ever nearer came the two pairs of fiendish eyes, nearer and ever nearer the vaguely defined bodies of the hyænas. Eager whines, breaking into horrible human-like laughs, burst from their ravenous throats. But a little more whetting of the appetite, a little more assurance that they might approach with impunity, and they would spring upon their prey. What was there to prevent them ? What indeed ? Only a little M-Chaga maiden, scarcely more than a child, on whose knees lay cradled a wounded mzungu, all-unconscious of his threatening doom.

CHAPTER XXI.

KATE never knew how that fateful journey across the Njiri plain was accomplished. At first she felt neither weariness nor terror. In a stupor of grief she plunged blindly on, Gilmour's last good-bye ringing in her ears and heart, and shutting out all other consciousness of sound or sight or feeling. Once or twice Ferhani urged her to rest a while, but she only looked at him uncomprehendingly, and mechanically kept on her way. Ferhani saw with apprehension that she would soon exhaust herself. He grasped the arm he held more firmly, and, turning to Tubu, bade him take the other. It was then that Ulu, seizing her opportunity, slipped away to return to her master. The two men were not long in becoming aware of her flight. By a look they signalled to each other not to let Kate know, and, bent on securing their own safety, held steadily on.

At last Kate stumbled, and would have fallen had not Tubu and Ferhani supported her.

"Bibi, rest a little," they urged, setting her gently on the ground.

Kate made no resistance, no remonstrance—simply lay as she was placed, motionless, with eyes closed. At length she looked up—looked round.

"Where is Ulu?" she asked with a start, as she suddenly missed the girl.

Ferhani and Tubu looked at each other guiltily. For a moment neither spoke.

"She has gone back to the Bwana," said Ferhani at last, selecting what he considered the least alarming explanation of Ulu's disappearance. In reality, both he and Tubu believed that she had sunk down exhausted, and by this time had become a prey to the hyænas.

Kate buried her face in her hands. "Oh, she is better than I," she moaned; "more faithful, more loving. Come, Ferhani," she added eagerly, as she struggled to her feet; "let us go back, too. We may yet be in time to help him."

"Impossible, bibi. We should all be killed," exclaimed the men in one breath.

"Cowards!" cried Kate, with an accent of ineffable contempt. "Then I shall go myself."

"Bibi, you cannot," said Ferhani, resolutely. "You do not know the way; you would only be eaten by the hyænas."

Kate looked wildly around. She had taken no

note of the way they had come. There was no
landmark to guide her. On every side the fitful
moonbeams revealed only a barren waste of shining
sand. The air was filled with the cries of wild
beasts. What Ferhani said seemed only too
true.

" Besides, we could not reach the Bwana in
time," the man continued in self-justification.
" In an hour it will be daylight." This was not
strictly true ; but the men were now bent on saving
their lives at any cost, and they dreaded any attempt
on Kate's part that might hinder their speedily
reaching a place of safety. Indeed, they were only
prevented from deserting her now by the fear of
what the consequences might be should the Bwana
ever again reach Pepo-ni.

Kate wrung her hands despairingly. " Oh, will
no one do anything for him ? " she cried.

" Bibi, I'll tell you what we'll do," said Tubu
consolingly, touched by the sight of Kate's anguish.
" As soon as we reach the mountain, I shall
hasten forward to Mkuyuni, and the malaam,
your father, will send out men to seek for the
Bwana ; that is," he added hastily, seeing how
Kate's face, which had brightened a little on her
hearing that he had some suggestion to offer,
fell again as she learned its unsatisfactory nature
—" that is, supposing the Bwana does not over-

take you, or reach the station before you by another way."

Once more Kate put her arm within Ferhani's, and resumed her way in the silence of utter despair. Every step was now an effort, and more than once it seemed as if she would break down altogether. At length, after many halts, the base of the mountain was gained, shortly after sunrise. Tubu and Ferhani breathed more freely. They were among friendly tribes, and their safety was assured.

Kate was indifferent. She did not care whether she died or lived. With horror she thought of the unequal conflict that even then might be raging on that little hill in the desert. Already, perhaps, Tom might be dead or dying, those black, hideous faces bending over him in fiendish glee. The thought was maddening, and Kate pressed wildly forward, in desperate effort seeking to keep it at bay.

In about an hour they reached a village, and there Kate dropped down exhausted. Willing hands carried her to a hut, where she was cared for with rude kindness. The bibi of Mkuyuni was well known throughout the length and breadth of Chaga for her goodness towards the sick, and her skill in healing them. The natives were glad to have an opportunity of showing they were not ungrateful.

After she had recovered somewhat, Kate drank a little milk. Soon afterwards she fell asleep. When she awoke it was afternoon. Her first request was for Tubu; but the man, mindful of his promise, had already started on his way to the mission station.

Taking leave of her simple friends, Kate once more resumed her way in company with Ferhani. All that night and part of next morning they journeyed on, Kate preferring, since rest she must, to rest during the heat of the day and travel by night. On the morning of the third day they were met by the search party sent by Tubu from Pisgah. Needless to say, Mr. Kennedy—impatient to meet his daughter—was at its head. In all the rapturous joy of that meeting, Kate never for a moment forgot her sorrow. As she lay with her head pillowed on her father's bosom, her arms about his neck, the first faint words she sobbed out were of Gilmour.

"Oh, papa—Tom—Mr. Gilmour—he is killed, and it was for me."

The missionary clasped his daughter closer in his arms. He had already heard the story of Gilmour's sacrifice from Tubu.

"Kate—my child," he said brokenly, "you do not know. Please God he will yet be restored to us safe and well."

But Kate did not hear. She only clung to her father, weeping, unconscious of everything save that this man who had died for her had loved her, and that she had rejected his love. Ah, she knew now that she loved him, taught by the agony of these last two days and nights. Oh, the anguish of the thought that now she could never atone to him for the pain she had given—that now he could never know the depth of aching affection within her— affection whose pent-up fulness seemed as if it must break her sorrowing heart.

For some time Mr. Kennedy let Kate's grief have its way. At length, gently disengaging her arms, he begged her to lie down, making a pillow for her of a rug which he carried. Kate yielded, after having given some direction to the men who were to go in search of Gilmour, and seen them safely despatched. There was no need to hurry now, so all that day and night Kate rested. She wished, indeed, to remain where she was until the mission men returned from their quest, clutching eagerly at the hope her father kept constantly before her mind, that Gilmour might, after all, have escaped with his life, though, if wounded, he could not have travelled so fast even as she had done, and there- fore could not possibly have been heard of. Mr. Kennedy, however, was anxious to get her home at once, particularly as he had himself but little faith in the hope he held out to his daughter, and he dreaded the return of his men with bad news or none. Accordingly, he earnestly urged Kate to continue her homeward journey. Kate suffered herself to be persuaded. Next day she wearily set out again, and late the same evening reached the mission station.

Three days elapsed, and still there was no news of the search party. A fourth passed, and Kate gave up all hope of its return that day.

It was late in the evening. Kate had gone to the porch to take a last wistful look along the path by which the men should have come. There was no one to be seen.

Suddenly, there was a sound of voices—a word or two of greeting. The men had returned. Had they found Gilmour? Kate dared not go to meet them—she could scarcely breathe. Yes, they had come. There were figures now advancing along the path. Kate counted them. One—two—three —four—five—six—only six! They had not found him, then! With a kind of fascination Kate stood gazing till the foremost man almost reached her. Then she turned and fled to her room. What need had *she* to hear his message? There was no hope now—none—none! Stunned and helpless, she sank down by her bedside, with clasped hands and face buried in the counterpane, wildly repeating to herself in an agonized whisper, "Tom! My darling! No hope! No hope!"

By-and-by her father came to her. He spoke no word of comfort, asked no explanation. Already he had guessed the secret of Kate's love. Gently the good man took his daughter's icy hand; gently he stroked her hair, and kissed her bowed head. But Kate neither moved nor spoke. The missionary grew alarmed.

"Kate, my darling," he whispered, "trust in God. Do not yet despair."

Kate raised her head wearily. Her eyes were bloodshot, her face wan and haggard. "They have not found him," she said, in a tone of reproach that seemed to ask, "Is not that enough?"

It was too true. They had not found him, nor any trace of him. The missionary had no consolation to offer. In silence he sat by his daughter for an hour or more, holding her hand in his. At last he rose. This mute, tearless grief was terrible to witness. He called her by every tender name he could think of, urging her to rouse herself, to be comforted. In vain. Kate seemed to be turned to stone.

"Papa, dear, if you would only leave me alone," was all she said.

Tenderly Mr. Kennedy raised her and laid her on the bed. He covered her with a warm rug, and kissed her again and again. Then he left her.

Through all that night, Kate never closed her eyes. The lamp burned low and went out; the dawn stole dimly into the darkened room, and filled it with a cold greyness; then the sun rose, once more bringing light and gladness to the earth. Not to Kate. To her no sun would ever again bring gladness. Oh, how could it shine there so pitilessly, smiling upon her grief!

Slowly she rose and arranged her dress. Once or twice she shivered, and the hope sprang up within her that she might take fever and die. All that day and for many days after she lived in a dull dream of sorrow—knowing nothing and caring nothing for what went on about her; her life grown hopeless, dead.

One morning Kate awoke, feeling almost light-hearted. She had dreamed that she was back again on Dónyo Erók, that Gilmour was with her, and that they were united by the mutual happiness of a mutual love, such, indeed, as they had never really known. Tom had called her "Kitty, dear," and was holding her hand when she awoke.

The change to stern reality at first seemed but as one of the startling changes in a dream, and for a moment Kate lay expecting that her room's familiar walls would vanish, and that she would awake to find herself in the little hut under the trees on the mountain-side. Suddenly there flashed upon her the recollection of the truth, and for the first time since all hope had deserted her, Kate wept. It was a great relief, and at breakfast that morning Mr. Kennedy noted with pleasure that if his daughter was not more cheerful, she was at least more resigned. For the first time since her return to Pisgah, he thought he might venture to leave her for a day, to pay a long overdue visit to an outlying station.

Two hours after her father had gone, Kate was sitting alone in the porch. Once more she was indulging in "the luxury of tears," her head bowed on her hands.

"Bibi, come; the Bwana wants you," suddenly said a voice behind her.

Kate started to her feet. Was she awake, or was she dreaming again? The voice was Ulu's.

No dream this time, Kate. It is Ulu who speaks, Ulu who stands beside you, looking ill and travel-stained—the shadow of her former graceful, supple self.

Kate had no time to note the change. "Ulu!" she gasped, almost fainting with joy. "How did you get here? Where have you come from? Where is he?"

"At Taveta. He is sick. He calls for you."

Kate did not wait to hear more. What mattered it to her how sick she was?—if only he lived it was joy enough for her. Gently she pushed Ulu towards the chair from which she had risen, and breathlessly hastened off to send a servant to her with some refreshment. Then she called together half a dozen men, and bade them prepare to accompany her to Taveta. When she returned she observed that the good things she had sent to Ulu still stood untasted.

"Eat, Ulu, eat," she eagerly urged; "we must start immediately, you know."

But Ulu was too ill to be hungry. She only drank a little milk and nibbled at a biscuit.

Kate was soon ready. Hastily pencilling a note to her father to tell him the glad news of Gilmour's safety, and bid him follow her to Taveta, she took Ulu by the hand, and together they set out towards the place where Gilmour lay.

As they went along, Kate gathered the story of the Masai attack and defeat—heard how Uledi was killed and Gilmour wounded; how he had wandered delirious over the desert; and how, guarded by Ulu, he had sunk down at length to die. Then Ulu told how all night she had watched over him, keeping off the hyænas, even shooting one with Gilmour's revolver. In the morning a Swahili caravan appeared in the distance—the very caravan which had hastened their flight from Dónyo Erók. Once more hope revived in Ulu's heart, and she fired the revolver to attract attention. Her efforts were successful. The traders halted, heard her story, and, believing that Gilmour was a person of importance, and that they would be well rewarded for their trouble, took him up and carried him with them to Taveta. There he had lain ever since. Sometimes the fever left him; but once and again it had returned, until he was now in the last stage of weakness.

Kate's gratitude to Ulu knew no bounds; but deeper than her gratitude was her anxiety for Gilmour, and faster and faster she hurried on, sure that her presence would work the speediest cure.

Ulu was very weary. It was hard work for her to keep pace with Kate's buoyant step—under the broiling sun, too, which Kate, in her impatience, did not seem to feel. Fortunately, the road was for the most part shady, and the poor little savage struggled bravely on. At length she felt herself giving way. Her head swam—she could not see the pathway in front of her. Gradually she lagged behind. Already Taveta lay in sight. Kate was lost in a happy dream of the coming meeting. Not until she was close to the forest village did she notice that Ulu no longer followed her. Conscience-stricken, she was about to turn back, but remembering how perhaps Gilmour lay at the point of death, and believing that, at the worst, Ulu was only very tired, she contented herself with sending two of her men, and herself hurried on through the wood.

It was late in the afternoon. The last rays of the setting sun lit up the huts of the traders' encampment with a ruddy glow. Eagerly Kate asked her way to the hut in which Gilmour lay. She bade her men remain behind—she would enter alone. For a moment she paused on the threshold, her eyes intently devouring the loved features of the invalid, as he lay on a low camp bedstead, apparently asleep. How pale and ill he looked! One wasted hand lay on the coverlet. Kate's eye filled with tears as she saw how white and thin it was. She stole noiselessly to the bedside, and gazed at Gilmour long and earnestly, fearful of waking him. Slowly his eyes opened.

"Kate!"

"My darling!"

Not another word was spoken. Kate sank on her knees by the side of the bed, and, seizing the poor, wasted hand, kissed it again and again. Another moment, and Gilmour, strong in a strength that was born of joy and hope, had raised himself on the pillow and drawn Kate towards him. Their lips met in the first sweet kiss of love.

For long—they knew not how long—they sat in silence, holding each other's hands. The hut grew dim with the quickly deepening darkness of the tropical twilight. Suddenly there was a sound of footsteps outside. Some one darkened the doorway for a moment, and the next, one of the mission men stood in the hut, bearing in his arms the unconscious form of Ulu. He laid her gently on the ground. Kate darted to her side in an agony of misgiving.

"Ulu, speak—what is it?" she cried, tenderly putting her arm under the girl's drooping head. "Are you hurt? Are you ill?"

Ulu opened her eyes. Already they seemed to be glazing in death.

"Bibi, come; the Bwana wants you," she said faintly.

Poor child! she remembered her message even in death. Gilmour struggled to rise, but sank back exhausted on his pillow. There was a fearful sickness at Kate's heart. Tenderly she pressed the little Mshenzi to her bosom.

"My little mtoto —— " she began, in a voice that was choked with tears.

Ulu looked up at her wistfully, wonderingly. "Ah, you have come," she said; "the Bwana will not be sick any more. You will marry him now, and you will be his chief wife, because an mzungu like himself, and I will be the next because first married. Oh, the Bwana is so good, so rich ——" she murmured. Then she abruptly stopped. For a moment a great light illumined her eyes as they fell upon Gilmour. "Bwana!" she cried, stretching her head eagerly towards him, "Bwana!"

There was a great sigh, a quick sudden sob from Kate, and Ulu fell back in her loving arms—dead!

THE END.

LONDON: PRINTED BY WILLIAM CLOWES AND SONS, LIMITED,
STAMFORD STREET AND CHARING CROSS.